MᴄCᴀʙᴇ's Lᴀw

Also by Patrick Lindsay

Opening the Frontier: Spencer and Son

Texas Rangers Stone & McKinnon

Chance Reilly Series

Chance Reilly

Gibson's Gold

Agua Caliente Canyon

Latigo Series

Latigo's Choice: Taming the West

Latigo's Chance: Boomtown Gold

Latigo's Trouble: Meltdown in Leadville

McCabe's Law

Jake McCabe
Book Two

Patrick Lindsay

WOLFPACK
PUBLISHING
— EST 2013 —

McCabe's Law

McCabe's Law

CHAPTER 1

FIRST BANK OF CRABAPPLE

MAY, 1873—NEAR FREDERICKSBURG, TEXAS

I squatted down behind the woodpile, muttering to myself as the afternoon sun beat down on me. I stared at the ramshackle wooden building across the street. A sign swung crookedly from the post on the left of the front doors, announcing that this was the First Bank of Crabapple, Texas. I let out a little snort and muttered to myself some more. Callin' that pile of wood a bank was a real stretch.

Sweat trickled down into my eyes and I wiped it away with the bandana that hung around my neck. I stared through my little peephole in the woodpile and waited for the guy robbing that bank over there to stick his head out through the door again.

I stared over at the brand-new Winchester '73 in the scabbard over there on my horse. Sherman, that's what I named the horse after the war. That was a mighty fine rifle over there, and if I hadn't tied him to the rail, I could have called Sherman right over here. Too late for that now. I had my Colt .45, and that would have to be enough.

A shot slammed into the woodpile and kicked up enough dust to blind me for a couple seconds. I wiped at my eyes with my bandana again and fired a shot through the peephole just to keep him from gettin' away before I could see.

I couldn't decide if this was good luck or bad. As sheriff of Gillespie County, I made a trip now and then to the other towns in the county. Mostly, I stayed around Fredericksburg, and that's where I lived. I had swung through Crabapple today, stopping to check in with a few folks. I had picked up a few things for my fiancée, Julia, in the general store. That's when a couple shots rang out from the bank.

My name is Jake McCabe, and I've been sheriff in this county for a little over a year. Today was the first time I'd been in a shootout since I'd had to face up to a gunfighter named Al Vincent a while back. I had to hope this guy wasn't as salty as Vincent. I carried a few aches and pains every time it rained on account of that little dustup back in Fredericksburg.

There were a couple more shots slamming into the woodpile now, but he didn't have me pinned down. He was spacing his shots up and down the pile, trying to draw me out. I could tell he wasn't sure where I was. I stared across the street at the hitching rail in front of the bank. There were three horses out there. I had to believe at least one of them belonged to the gunman. Trouble was, I didn't know if there was more than one of 'em over there.

I decided to wait him out. The shots he was sendin' over here told me to stay still. I didn't need to give him any clues. Sooner or later, he had to come out of there. I shoved a couple more rounds into my Colt and waited.

It was another fifteen minutes before he moved. I was eyeballing my Winchester again, over there in the saddle, when the front door of the bank came flyin' open and he bolted out the door, carrying a sack in one hand and sprayin' shots in my general direction.

I stood as he reached the front of the porch, lifted my Colt, and fired just once. The shot drilled him through the heart. He dropped the burlap sack he was carrying and pitched forward toward the street.

He bounced off the bottom step and came to rest in front of the hitching rail. I was still staring at him when there was a sharp sting across my right shoulder. I dropped the Colt and spun backward, which probably saved my life. Another shot whistled through the space where I'd just been and buried itself into the wall of the general store behind me.

I dropped to my knees, picked up the Colt, and crawled back to my peephole in the woodpile. The second guy was holding a woman in front of him, dragging her toward the hitching rail. He was just watching and waitin' for me to stick my fool head up over the woodpile. I waited.

Finally, he shoved the woman away and leaped into the saddle in one move. He fired another shot in my direction and wheeled his horse around. I stood as he spurred his horse and fired a quick shot at him. He grabbed his shoulder and dropped the burlap sack he was carrying, but stayed in the saddle and raced toward the edge of town.

I fired another shot from the Colt, but it didn't stop him. I raced over to Sherman and pulled the Winchester, lifted it, and sighted on the guy just as he reached a bend in the road. I fired once and saw him hunch a little more in the saddle, but then he was gone.

Taking a quick look at the robber I'd dropped at the foot of the stairs, I could see he wasn't goin' anywhere. I wheeled around and started back toward Sherman, but then there were hands reaching at me from everywhere. The woman who'd been shoved down in the street grabbed me from behind.

"Sheriff!" she shouted. "Where are you going?"

I pointed toward the escaping robber, but she grabbed me and hung on. "You stay here!" she demanded.

The owner/manager of what passed for a bank was in front of me, blocking the way to my horse. "They have robbed my bank!" he shouted.

I looked over his shoulder at what he was callin' a bank. He had hauled a safe into a shack and folks left some money with him ever' now and then, so I guess he could call it a bank if he wanted to. It wasn't no bigger than my barn back home, and there was room for more'n two horses in there. Okay, maybe three.

I sighed and walked back toward the bank. I picked up the sacks dropped by both robbers and gave them to the bank manager. The woman was still sobbing and holding on to my sleeve.

"Ma'am, are you hurt?" I asked. If she gave me an answer, I couldn't tell. I sighed and looked over her shoulder, where I saw a man coming out of a building, carrying a black bag.

"Are you a doctor?" I shouted.

He nodded, and I gently turned the woman around to face him. "Please check her out, Doc," I asked. He nodded and took her over to sit down on a bench.

The bank manager was still in my face. "... had a lot of money in the safe today!" he was shouting.

I steered him back into the bank and sat him down. He was still holding the two bags. "Count those," I told him, "And then tell me if anything is missing." I wasn't sure what he considered a lot of money to be, and I didn't feel like asking.

I trotted back out to the street and stared down at the man I had shot. I knelt and inspected his face. I was sure I'd never seen him before. A few townspeople had drifted pretty close to the body, so I stood and backed them off.

"Give it some room, folks," I told them.

I trotted back into the bank, which was empty now except for the manager. He had the money spread out, and he'd written down a few numbers on a sheet of paper. I waited while he added them up.

"Well?" I asked.

"Looks like they didn't get nuthin'," he mumbled.

"I'll be back," I told him. I trotted back outside and headed for my horse again.

The doctor stopped me. "Your arm," he said, pointing.

I looked down and was surprised to see a lot of blood on my sleeve. Once I saw it, a throb started up. I tore the shirt sleeve open and turned toward the doctor.

"Is it bad?" I asked.

He looked it over and shook his head. "Not too bad," he allowed. "But I need to stitch you up a little."

"I'll be back," I told him. I pointed at the corpse in the street and announced loudly: "Nobody moves him. Leave 'im there until I get back." With that, I mounted Sherman and took the main road out of town.

I knew he had at least a ten-minute lead on me now. I nudged Sherman up to a trot as we reached the edge of town. There were drops of blood on the trail, and I didn't want to move any faster. If he had turned off into the trees on either side, I couldn't afford to ride past it on the first pass.

Several minutes passed, and I could still see the tracks and the occasional drops of blood on the trail. I'd scored at least a couple hits on him. I wasn't sure if he was strong enough to travel very far.

The sound of rushing water reached me after another couple of minutes, and I had a sinking feeling I knew what he had done. The tracks led off the trail and into a small stream rushing past on the west side. He had ridden his horse into the stream and followed it. The trail disappeared under the moving water.

I rode along in the stream for a few minutes, hoping to see tracks leading up onto the stream bank, but this guy was no fool. He had stayed in the water. After a few minutes, I heaved a sigh of disappointment and turned Sherman back toward Crabapple.

The body lay where I'd left it, and I detoured to the doc's office to get patched up. Returning to the street, I squatted down on my haunches and took a long look at the robber. I'd never seen him before, I was sure. I fished around in his pockets and found no clues as to who he was.

I looked up to see the general store owner looking out from his shop. I crossed the street and pointed back at the corpse. "Who does your burial work around here?" I asked him.

He pointed down the street. "Barber shop," he

answered. "He has an area out back where he builds the coffins and then he buries 'em. Charge seven dollars apiece. Buries 'em out yonder." He pointed vaguely at a field a little out of town.

I moved down the street and made arrangements with the barber. I waited for a receipt for the seven dollars and stared across the street. Crossing over, I gathered up Sherman's reins and was about to saddle up when I thought of one more thing I wanted to check.

I moved back over to the body and stared at the belt buckle. It was a US Army buckle. I'd worn one of them myself during the war. On a hunch, I pulled the belt off him. Sometimes, before going into a heavy battle, soldiers had pinned their names to their shirts or scratched their names on the back of belt buckles so the Army could notify family if they were killed.

I flipped the buckle over and stared at the back of it. The words *Red Saunders* were scratched on the back. The name meant nothing to me, but at least I knew who he was. I stuffed the belt into my saddlebag and left town.

———

The belt buckle stayed in my mind as I took the trail back home to Fredericksburg. I was one of very few folks around here who had fought for the Union. I didn't advertise it much, but I told folks when asked. Kentucky, where I was from, was supposed to be a neutral state, but my pa and I had both suited up for the Union, and our neighbors didn't like it much.

This Billy Barber, I was guessing, was from up north somewhere. The number of people fighting for the North in the war was even smaller around here than it was up in Kentucky. I wondered if he had any friends who'd come down here with him to ride the outlaw trail. Maybe that other guy in the bank who was carrying my lead in him was another.

I had been sheriffin' in this county for a little over a year now, and this was the first robbery of any kind I'd run across, let alone a bank robbery. If there was a gang of robbers from up north, that was bad news for me. I heaved a sigh and clucked at Sherman to pick up the pace a bit.

Truth was, it looked like I might have my hands full with a range war brewing down south of Fredericksburg. A family named Swift had a spread south of town, and there was a beef between them and their neighbors to the west, a family named Hicks. I'd sent my deputy, Boone, out to the Swift spread today for a sit-down. When I got home, I was hoping to hear they were talking a little more sense down there.

My mood lifted as I got closer to home. I had a little land and some cows that I shared on a spread with a man named Ike Hawkins and his family. His daughter, Julia, was my fiancée. The Hawkins were good people. They'd been my friends when I'd plumb run out of family and friends back in Kentucky.

I glanced down at the bandage around my arm and swung my arm back and forth a little to test the stiffness. Julia would make a fuss over this. She worried about me being sheriff, especially since I'd been shot up pretty good a couple of years ago, before I pinned on the badge.

I topped the last rise and could see my little ranch house in the distance. It was good to be home, like always.

Julia Hawkins finished mopping the kitchen floor, carried the bucket out the back door, and tossed the water on her vegetable garden out back. She set the bucket down and looked back at the big stone ranch house where she now lived with her family. It still didn't seem quite real.

They had bought this house from the bank when the previous owner had left the state to escape the law. They owned the house and fourteen hundred acres of land, granted to her father as an injured Confederate veteran. Compared to the humble little shack and a few acres they had left behind in Kentucky, she felt rich now.

She heard the barn door shut behind her and turned to see her brothers Pete and Isaac coming toward the house. Pete was the older, nineteen now, and Isaac, the younger one, was seventeen. She watched them come and felt the worry start up inside her again about Pete. He was moody now in a way he never had been, and she could tell he wasn't happy working here on the ranch. She could feel how much it troubled her parents, who had risked everything when they left Kentucky and came here.

Isaac grinned on the way by, looking like his usual happy-go-lucky self. Pete passed her with barely a glance in her direction, caught up in his own thoughts, whatever those might be. Whatever was bothering Pete, she hadn't been able to find out. Her father Ike came out of the barn last, hobbling along on the crutch he had used ever since the war.

Ike stopped to give her a kiss on the cheek. "How're you doing, daughter of mine?" he boomed.

Julia smiled, as most people did when they were around Ike. She returned his hug and turned to walk to the house with him, but she noticed his eyes following Pete. There was worry in those eyes, and she hated to see it.

Julia stepped into the kitchen and dished up some of the roast her mother had prepared. Nobody raised an eyebrow—it was her custom to take dinner up to Jake's house for the two of them on the nights Jake didn't join them for dinner. She threw a towel over the dish and began her usual walk up to Jake's house.

Jake had originally built the house for the Hawkins family and had moved in only after they had claimed the ranch house on the adjoining property. Julia stopped to pick a few of the remaining spring wildflowers, then climbed the short embankment to Jake's house.

In some ways, she preferred this house to the big stone ranch house below. This one overlooked the pasture in between the houses and was surrounded by woods on both the east and west sides. Jake had dug a well at the foot of the embankment, and the house was well-positioned for defense. That had come in handy in the past.

Julia was a little surprised that Jake wasn't home already when she arrived—he had expected to be back around this time. She placed the wildflowers in a small vase she had bought for Jake, then occupied herself by sweeping out the cabin. She glanced out the door from time to time but saw no sign of him.

Forty-five minutes later, she felt the first touch of concern. The sheriff's job had been pretty routine so far, but she was still worried. With one more look out the door, she went back and set two plates on the table for them. She laid a little wood in the stove to start a fire to warm the food, then decided to wait. She wasn't sure when he would be back.

Julia moved a chair out to the porch and took a seat, remaining calm by choice. She wouldn't let herself worry about things she couldn't help. The sun was dipping behind the oak trees in the west when she finally heard hoofbeats on the trail.

She stood and watched, feeling some relief when she saw the dark hair and familiar red shirt coming down the trail. Jake didn't consider himself handsome, but Julia knew that her favorite sight was Jake coming home along that trail. He was, she decided, a guy who didn't know he was handsome. That was the best kind, as far as she was concerned.

She stood as he turned his horse into the yard. He was holding himself a little stiffly. Her glance traveled down to take in a large patch and a sling on his arm.

CHAPTER 2

THE ROOST

It was too early in the year for the 100-degree temperature stuff we got around here, but I still felt some powerful relief when the sun started sliding down in the west, taking that direct heat off me. I passed my good arm across my forehead and started wondering exactly how to explain this busted wing I had to Julia. The pain had settled down to a constant throb. The doc in Crabapple had said it would hurt for a few days. He said to see a doc in Fredericksburg to get the stitches out of me in about a week.

I reached the turnoff to my cabin, knowing Julia would wait for me at the cabin, and I was later than I'd expected. That wouldn't bother her, I knew. It was just the stopping bullets part she wouldn't like.

I walked Sherman down the path, past the post oaks shading the dusty trail. I turned into the yard and saw Julia sitting on the porch, just as I had expected. She stood with a big smile and came down the steps. Her eyes traveled down to my sling, and I heard the sharp intake of breath. I held up my good arm and waved.

"I'm fine," I said. I swung down off Sherman, using my good arm again, and walked him into my corral. "Just got winged a little," I said, feeling pretty sure I wasn't convincin' her much.

She hugged me on the good side and gave me a kiss. Her eyes stayed glued to my injured arm. "Is it broken?" she asked.

"Nope," I assured her. "Just took a flesh wound through the arm up at the top of the shoulder. Had a bank robbery going on in Crabapple, if you can believe that. Banker said he had a couple ranchers get paid off for some cows they sent up the trail to Kansas, brought their money to the bank. I guess somebody knew about that. Couple of somebodies."

She steered me into the cabin, holding on to my good arm, and sat me down in a chair. "I'll heat this roast and get you some dinner," she promised. After about twenty minutes in front of the stove, she set down a steaming plate, and I tucked into it. Maybe, I thought, getting shot perked up your appetite. I decided not to make that joke. Anyway, I didn't remember having a good appetite after getting shot last time. Must have been all that riding out to Crabapple and back that did it.

Julia waited while I finished off what I had on my plate, then dished out a little more. When I finally sat back, I knew it was time to explain what had happened. I described the two robbers in the bank, and how I'd been behind that woodpile, shooting it out. When I explained that I'd killed one man and maybe a second, she only nodded. Julia had done her share of defending herself.

I finished up telling her about the Union army belt buckle, and she didn't know what to make of that, either. "It's a long way down here for a Union vet," she observed.

"I wonder if he moved here like you to live in Texas, or he's just down here robbing."

She'd hit that nail on the head. "Been wondering the same thing," I said. I didn't mention we didn't need a bunch of renegade Union soldiers stirring up trouble down here. Quantrill and his boys had stirred up enough trouble up north of here, although they had been Confederate soldiers, at least for a while.

Julia came around the table and settled down in my lap. "I know you were careful," she said. "That's the promise you made to me when you took the sheriff's job. I can't ask more than that."

I nodded, and she stared at the tabletop. "What about the Texas State Police?" she asked. "Can you ask them for help?"

I shook my head instantly. "Poor reputation," I told her. "They had a captain that was probably murdering prisoners. Folks out west of here won't even let the state police arrest known criminals. Likely to cause me more harm than good."

She nodded unhappily, and we settled into silence. She wrapped an arm around my good side and we looked out the door as the sun set.

We heard a horse pull up outside, and I knew from the uneven sound of footsteps on the stairs outside that my father-in-law Ike had come for a visit. He had a wooden leg as a souvenir of the war.

"Stop yer canoodling," he boomed as he poked his head into the doorway. He waved a bottle of whiskey in the air. "I've come with a gift," he announced, at only slightly less volume.

I chuckled and waved him through the door while Julia stood and cleared a spot at the table. Ike plopped down, stretched out his wooden leg, and popped the cork on the whiskey bottle with his teeth. The popping noise echoed inside the cabin. Julia set the glasses down and Ike poured generously.

I grinned and took the glass he offered me. It was just what I needed for that dull ache I'd been feeling for the last three hours. The warmth from the first sip left a trail all the way down to my stomach.

Ike looked at my sling and raised his eyebrows in the air. I went through the whole explanation again.

"I said maybe the state police—" Julia began.

Ike shook his head back and forth vigorously. "Do you more harm than good," he announced. He reached for the bottle and poured refills. "I heard somethin' today, over at the general store, might help, though."

I waited. Ike liked to gather with some others around the stove at the general store, having coffee in the mornings. I learned a lot about what was going on around here from things Ike passed along.

"Heard the Texas Rangers is gettin' put back together," Ike said. "Folks like and trust the Rangers a lot more than the state police. Mebbe they'll help if things get out of hand. Bank robberies or range wars or whatever. You an' Boone—well, you're a couple of salty guys, but there's only the two of you."

I leaned back in my chair and let that one sink in for a minute. "You thinkin' I should join the Rangers?" I started. "Because they elected me here for two years and I—"

Ike shifted forward and waved his hand in the air to stop me. "Nope, not what I'm thinkin'," he declared. "I know you're a man of your word and you're for sure gonna serve out the two years as sheriff. That's a big part of why I like you and why folks around here like you. You're somebody who does what he says. I'm just sayin' you might go to them for some hep if'n you get into more'n you and Boone can handle."

I glanced over at Julia and she looked as surprised as I felt. As for Ike, he had just heard about it that day, so it looked like Julia didn't know about it either. She'd said more than once, though, that she wished I had more help available should anything turn ugly in this county.

I stared at the floor. "Most of them Ranger boys was Confederate in the war," I pointed out. "I was Union. Feelin's still run pretty strong in a lot of places. You think I could really go to 'em for help?"

Ike leaned forward and refilled his glass. He held the bottle out in my direction, but I covered my glass and shook my head. "Most of 'em are fair," Ike pointed out. "The war's over—you're all just here to keep the peace now. The good 'uns know you're fair and they'll hep you, all right." He downed the refill he'd just poured. "Something to keep in mind. I don't want my daughter over here to lose her husband afore she gets to the altar. I don't want to lose you, neither. You're family."

I glanced over at Julia again and was startin' to feel a little misty. It saved me from getting sloppy when I heard Boone stomping up the steps outside. "I'm thirsty," he bellowed before ducking into the cabin. His eyes lit up when he saw the bottle on the table.

Boone leaned his Sharps up against a corner and accepted the glass Julia poured for him. "Thanks, darlin'," he told her. He plopped down into a chair and put his feet up on the table. A frown from Julia caused him to drop them back on the floor. "Sorry, darlin'," he mumbled. "Lived in the back of a saloon for too long."

I waited for him to report on the situation at the Swift ranch. Boone downed his drink, looked up in my direction, and shook his head. "Don't look good," he said. "The Hicks clan, they wouldn't even come out to talk today. Said they didn't wanna talk to no depu-tee like me. They'll come if'n you show up down there, but I'm thinkin' they might come packin' iron. Could get real ugly in no time a'tall."

I ran a hand over my face and sighed. "What about Jeb Swift?" I asked. "What's he got to say?"

Boone snorted and shook his head. "Likes to think he's the old bull of the woods, he does. Likes to go around givin' orders and the Hicks boys don't cotton to getting orders from the likes of him. He was fumin' and bellering around down there when the Hicks didn't show. Wanted to know where you were." He glanced at me sideways. "I said I'd talk to you about comin' back down there with me tomorrow. Maybe we could pick up the Hicks boys on the way."

I nodded and stared out the door. "The beef they've got is about water, right?" I asked. "About a stream that runs through there and divides the property?"

Boone nodded. "That's right, except Old Man Swift don't agree it divides the property. He claims all of it an' drives the Hicks herd away when they come to water."

I got up and walked over to a table I used for a desk over in the corner of the room. I took some drawings and spread them out on the dinner table. Ike, Julia, and Boone all came over to look. "Got these at the county clerk's office the day before yesterday," I told them. "Shows real clearly on here that the water belongs to both of 'em."

Boone looked it over and then up at me. "Looks right to me," he announced. "What do you wanna do?"

"We'll go see them tomorrow," I said. "Old Jeb Swift is gonna' have to back off a bit, or else he might spend some time in my jail." I stared at Boone over the table. "We got to be prepared if he don't feel like cooperatin'."

Boone grinned and moved over to pick up his Sharps rifle. "I'll bring my shotgun along with this tomorrow," he promised. "Ol' Betsy has a way of convincing folks when I've got both barrels pointed their way."

Boone stopped in the doorway and pointed at my arm. "What's with the busted wing?" he asked.

I waved my good arm in the air. "Long story," I told him. "I'll tell you about it on the way down there tomorrow."

Ike picked up his bottle and his walking stick and headed for the door right behind Boone. "Time for me to get on home," he thundered. "I'll leave you young-uns to get back to yore canoodlin' over here."

"How do you know we were canoodling?" I shot back at him as he reached the door.

He stopped and turned back to look at me. "You sayin' you weren't?" he demanded.

I shrugged and Julia, standing behind me, chuckled.

"That's what I thought," he said. Moments later, we could hear his horse trotting out of the yard.

Julia came over and picked up where we left off, sitting in my lap.

"I thought maybe you and Ike had already talked about the Texas Rangers getting back together," I said.

She shook her head. "I guess he kept that one to himself when he came home today. You know I like Boone and I know he'll back you up in a fight. I just wish you had somewhere to go, or somebody to talk to if you get outnumbered. There's the Army, but folks don't trust the Union army a lot right now. Maybe in another ten or twenty years, but the war is a little too fresh."

I didn't say anything, but I had to admit it made sense to me to turn to the Rangers if I got in over my head. "If you hear anything more about them getting back together, let me know," I told her. "I promise I'll look into it."

She stood and walked with me to the door, where she gave me a kiss before leaving. "Be careful out at the Swift's place tomorrow," she said. "He's a stubborn old man."

———

Johnny Carr sat at what passed for the bar of a saloon in the tiny town of Becknell, New Mexico. It wasn't much, but it was more than he had anywhere else near the place he was building. The tent flaps snapped and waved in the stiff, dusty wind. Carr put one hand over his beer glass to keep the dust out.

Carr waved for another and allowed himself a small smile when he thought about the place he was building. He would put a saloon in there. Then he wouldn't need to ride out to this desolate place.

Not that his place was any less desolate than Becknell. It was actually only a few miles east of here, in a place they called the Public Land Strip or No Man's Land. Carr preferred No Man's Land. It didn't belong to any state or any territory, therefore it had no law. Perfect for a man like himself.

He knew the history of the place. He'd made a point

of finding out when he got out of the Union army after the war. Actually, he had left a little early with a few of the boys in his unit, but nobody had found them out. Lieutenant Carr had just disappeared.

Anyway, this No Man's Land had been formed in 1850, after something called *The Compromise of 1850* was passed. Texas had entered the Union as a slave state in 1845. The Compromise of 1850 said there couldn't be slavery north of the thirty-six degrees thirty minutes north parallel. And so, Texas had shaved off a piece of the state. It looked like the handle of a pan, sandwiched between Texas and Kansas, out there between Oklahoma and New Mexico. No laws. Carr grinned and downed another beer.

He'd taken five of his boys with him when he'd left the Army, and they had made some money, done some hard work, and stolen more money to make a rock fortress in a place he was calling the *Robber's Roost*. There were other folks who had claimed to have a Robber's Roost here and there, but Carr didn't care. It suited his place just fine.

They had built, or paid some people to build, a big rock house on a long prominent ridge, right out on the westernmost piece of No Man's Land. It commanded an excellent field of fire and they could see people coming for miles. It was pretty handy to the Cimarron Cutoff of the Santa Fe Trail. He and the boys could always steal a few cows and a couple horses from stragglers on the trail, then disappear into the Roost.

There was a deep canyon just northeast of the rock house where they could hide the cows for a few weeks. The canyon backed up against a steep rock face, with just one narrow, winding trail leading out. The stolen livestock were safe as babies back there. He and the boys had become experts at hiding the original brands, and they could always sell the cows to cattle drives moving north. The good horses they'd stolen, they kept for themselves. The rest they gave to the Cherokee warriors, just to keep them happy. It wasn't really Cherokee land, but a few stolen horses meant they didn't have to worry about war parties.

Carr stepped to the edge of the beer tent and squinted at the sun overhead. It was time to get on back to the Roost. He had split up his gang and sent them on two separate raids. Two of them, Harris and Wood, had gone to the Cimarron Cutoff to steal a few more cows.

The other two, Finn and Red, had gone south to try something new. Carr was a little worried about pulling too many robberies along the Santa Fe Trail. If they caused too much trouble, the Army might come after them. The rock fortress at the Roost could hold off most attacks, but the Army had cannons. They didn't need that kind of trouble.

He had sent Finn and Red down into Texas to rob a couple of places. Preferably banks, but he'd left that up to Finn and Red. Carr had just made it clear he expected to see some gold when they got back.

He stepped into the saddle and took the trail home. One man, Dennison, had been left to keep an eye on the place. Dennison was his right-hand man, and a good man with his gun. Truth was, Dennison was the only one he'd be scared to pick a fight with.

An hour later, Carr was back at the Roost. He rode up to see Harris and Wood unsaddling out front. Carr walked over, folded his arms, and got right down to it.

"How many cows have we got over in the canyon now?" he demanded.

Both men had their eyes on the ground. Finally, Harris lifted his eyes to look at Carr. "None," he answered, "they seemed to be waiting for us."

Carr stared at him icily and let the silence build.

Harris glanced over at Wood, then lifted his arms in the air. "There was just one wagon and four or five cows, looked like they'd fallen behind the wagon train by a mile or two. Easy pickin's, that's what we thought. We rode up an' they lifted the flap of that wagon and cut loose at us. Four or five of 'em in the wagon. Caught a crease across the side, I did." He pointed at a bloody streak just above his belt.

Carr felt the angry red flush rising in his cheeks. He doubled up his fist, stepped forward, and swung just one punch. Harris collapsed to the ground. Carr turned and strode into the rock house. He hated bad news.

CHAPTER 3

FINN LONIGAN

Morning gray was just showing in the east when I heard Boone clomping up my steps. His moods in the morning were even worse than mine, so I just nodded at him and shoved the coffeepot and a cup in his direction. He helped himself and slumped into a chair at my table, propping his boots up and slurping. He put his feet down and straightened up when he heard Julia riding into the yard.

It was going to be a three-hour ride this morning by the time we swung by the Hicks ranch to make sure they would come to the powwow this morning, so we tucked into the breakfast Julia brought over. I could only imagine how early she must have been up, getting it ready. I wondered for about the hundredth time how I had gotten this lucky. Boone told me on a regular basis he couldn't figure it out, either. He was just jealous, I was sure of that.

We struck the trail for the Hicks ranch, not talking for the first half hour or so. I glanced over at Boone's saddle, the shotgun and Sharps were both in there.

"Do you think it's a shootin' war?" I asked finally.

Boone stuck a toothpick between his lips and shrugged. "I'd say it's about fifty-fifty," he growled. "Old man Hicks don't want one, neither does Jeb Swift, he just likes to push folks around. The wild card is two of the kids. Zach Swift and Caleb Hicks. Zach Swift thinks he's pretty good with his fists, an' he'd like to get in a rumble. Caleb Hicks might be more dangerous. Fancies himself with a gun. If he crows any louder, Jeb Swift might hire hisself a gun hand. Then we'd have some real trouble."

Boone lapsed into silence, seeing as how that was just about the longest speech I'd ever heard him give.

I puzzled over what he'd told me. "Do you really think Swift would hire a gun hand?" I asked.

Boone shrugged again. "Don't know. I'm just guessin'. Jeb Swift don't want to take water in front of no man, and Caleb Hicks has a big mouth. Might be too late to cool this off," he added moodily.

Zeke Hicks, the old man of the family, was standing at the gates when we rode up. I glanced behind him, two of his three sons were saddled up to go. Adam, the oldest, was the rancher and cattleman of the sons. The other one at the gate was Caleb, as I'd feared. He wore double tied-down guns around his waist and a smirk on his mouth.

I took in the three of them and spoke to Zeke, but my eyes were on Caleb. "This is a peaceful trip," I emphasized to Zeke. "Don't none of us need a shootin' war or range war of any kind around here."

Zeke nodded and looked around at his boys. "Peaceful trip," he repeated. The smirk never left Caleb's face.

We settled into a stony silence on the way over to the Swift's ranch. Zeke rode beside me with a sour face and nothing to say. His boys trailed behind us and Boone brought up the rear, much to Caleb's irritation. He turned around a time or two and glared at Boone, but that shotgun was never too far out of reach. Funny, I thought, how a shotgun can keep things quiet.

We fanned out in a half-circle outside the Swift's ranch house when we arrived. Jeb Swift and his son Zach, the one who fancied himself a fighter, were in the middle. A couple hands sat on the left and right, and in the back was a guy I'd never seen before, but I knew trouble when I looked at it. Boone drifted off to the side, covering my flank.

I pointed at the guy behind Jeb Swift. "Never saw him before," I told Jeb. "Who's he?"

"New hand," was all Swift said. The guy in the back stared at me, no expression at all on his face. I wasn't even sure the guy knew how to blink. I had a feeling it wasn't just from playing a lot of poker. It looked like maybe it was too late to keep Swift from hiring a paid gun.

"He got a name?" I asked.

Swift leaned over and spat. "Cade," he said.

"First name or last name?" I asked.

Jeb Swift shrugged. "Don't know. I just call him Cade."

This wasn't getting me anywhere. I pulled the maps I got from the county clerk from my saddlebag. "Let's make this a short meetin'," I suggested. I waved the plans in the air. "These here are the original maps from the sale of these ranches, showing the property you each own. The creek over yonder cuts right between 'em, meaning both of you have equal access to the water. Either of you tries to cut the other off, you'll answer to me."

Jeb Swift's eyes narrowed, and he stared at me. I

suspected nobody had ever talked to him like that. I locked eyes with him and stared him down. Zach Swift started his horse forward and the gun hand in back slid his right hand down ever so slowly.

Boone cocked both barrels and cleared his throat loudly. "Ol' Betsy here," he announced, "has two barrels, and she don't care which saddle she empties first. After that, I've got this here Sharps, and it's full of bullets. On top of that, my nerves ain't as good as they used to be. I get twitchy sometimes, I do."

Jeb Swift eased back just slightly and held out a hand, palm down, to tell his men to back off. He chewed his wad of tobacco and leaned over to spit. "Okay, Sheriff," he said, forcing the calm in his voice. "Looks like you've got the upper hand."

Zach Swift edged his horse forward. "Think you can back up them words without the guns?" he asked.

"I can," I told him.

He snorted.

"What size are those britches you're wearing?" I asked him.

He stared at me, confused. "I dunno," he said.

"Well," I told him. "I'd suggest the next time you buy britches, you buy 'em a couple sizes smaller. You're not nearly big enough to wear those."

Even Swift's hands were smiling at that one, and I heard a few chuckles from Hicks and his sons. Boone was clearly enjoying it the most. When I looked at Zach Swift, I knew there was a knuckle-and-skull fight in my future, but I'd figured on that. Time for the boy to grow up a little.

I stayed and kept talkin' until Swift and Hicks shook hands and said they'd share the water. They weren't looking at each other, so I wasn't sure how much good I'd done. Zach Swift would have started a fight with me right there if his daddy hadn't stopped him.

We eased away from the ranch and said goodbye to Zeke Hicks, who seemed happy enough with the meeting. I couldn't speak for his boy Caleb, though. There was trouble in those eyes. I knew I could settle Zach Swift's hash by takin' him down to size if he challenged me to a fistfight. Caleb Hicks, though—that boy wanted to pull those pistols.

Boone and I took the road back to Fredericksburg. I planned to spend the afternoon in the sheriff's office there. Boone rode along and started chuckling.

"That boy plumb hates you. Don't you get in a fight with Zach Swift if I ain't there to see it," he demanded. "I made some good money bettin' on your last fight around here. Tougher man than Zach Swift, too. Old Bull what's-his-name. You whupped him good." He chortled again. "Yup," he mused to himself, "made some good money on that'un."

"I'm gettin' older," I reminded Boone. "Maybe he'll beat me."

Boone snorted. "He don't know a thing about boxing, like you do, I'll wager. He probly just swings from the heels and hopes for the best. I don't know if anybody will bet on him, though." He frowned. "I'm gonna have to find some suckers who ain't seen you fight before."

"Life is hard," I told him. We parted ways when I went to the office and Boone tied up his horse in front of the saloon.

———

The argument on the back porch was loud and getting louder. Julia could only hear bits and pieces of it, but Ike and Pete were at it again. Julia could hear Ike talking about ranch duties and wanting Pete to hold up his end of the bargain. Pete yelled something back about making his own choices. Finally, the barn door slammed and Pete rode past the window toward Fredericksburg.

Julia eased out the back door and took a seat in the rocker next to her dad. One look at Ike told her that his rocker was taking a beating. Ike muttered to himself, pushing the rocker back and forth as hard as he could with his one good leg.

Finally, Ike slowed down and turned to look at Julia, pain and frustration clear on his face. "What's the matter with Pete?" he asked, spreading his hands and pointing out at their land. "And what's wrong with this ranch? It's the best thing that ever happened to this family. We fought for it. We..." Ike slowed down, stopped talking, then finally went back to rocking.

Julia chose her words carefully. "This was your dream, coming here. I love it, too. Mom wasn't sure at first, but now it's home for her. She loves it too. And Isaac, well, Isaac is going to be the best rancher of all of us. Like a duck to the water, that's Isaac on this ranch."

Ike nodded his head vigorously while she talked, waiting to hear something about Pete. Julia stopped and stared out across the pasture.

"And Pete?" Ike demanded. "Why isn't this good enough for Pete?"

Julia weighed her words carefully. "It's not about this place not being good enough. I think...well, I think Pete just might not want to be a rancher."

Ike slumped in his chair, baffled. "If he's not a

rancher, then what is he? This is our place. This is the future for all of us. We all agreed on that when we came here from Kentucky."

"Yes, we did," Julia agreed. "But Pete was only sixteen when we came here. It was a big adventure. None of us really knew what it would be like. Now, he's been here three years, he's worked on the ranch. Maybe this isn't what he wants."

"If he's not a rancher, what is he? What's he gonna do?"

Julia hesitated. "He likes to go around with Jake, making his rounds as sheriff. Pete seems to like that."

Alarmed, Ike shook his head vigorously. He pointed at his knee. "One wooden leg is all this family needs. Jake's a man. Pete's a boy. I won't have him gettin' hisself shot following Jake around."

Julia said nothing and sat quietly, waiting.

Ike slumped down into his chair, shaking his head. After a moment, Julia got up to leave. She knew Ike would think about the things she had said, and she'd said enough for one day. A request from Ike stopped her at the door.

"I don't know where he goes or what he does when he rides off to Fredericksburg. I know he's nineteen now and I guess it's his life, but I worry about him. Your mother worries about it more than me. Can you find out where he's going and make sure he's not in any trouble? I need to know that."

Julia nodded. She had been thinking about doing just that. Pete didn't spend all of his free time following Jake around. Maybe it was time to find out where else he was going. "I'll do it," she said softly.

Finn Lonigan was hurting. He'd been shot twice by a sheriff back there in a place called Crabapple, Texas. He snorted at the ridiculousness of it. His old lieutenant, Johnny Carr, had told them to go down and find the easiest money they could find in Texas. And they'd found it! Well, they thought so anyway. They hadn't bothered to wait for Carr.

Lonigan and his best buddy from the Army, Red Saunders, had wandered into a saloon in this place called Crabapple, Texas, and they'd heard two drunk ranchers talking about how much money they'd been paid for cattle driven up to Kansas. And they had put the money in a homemade bank you could probably push over with one good shove.

Then, somehow, this local sheriff had shown up and opened fire on them when they were leaving the bank. He'd cut down Red with one shot from his pistol, then he'd put two bullets into Finn, probably with his rifle.

Finn leaned over and coughed. He was coughing up blood now. Nobody had to tell him that was a bad sign. He had to find a doctor. He had ridden as far as he could from Crabapple. Now he had to find a doctor and get some rest. He had reached the first meeting point. Maybe help would come.

He and Red had agreed on two places where Johnny Carr could come and meet them. They'd already pulled off the robbery, but Carr was still supposed to come down here. Finn pulled his horse over, leaning across the saddle horn. The big suspension bridge was in front of him. That meant he had reached Waco. In another day or two, Johnny Carr would come through town, looking for them. That was what they'd agreed on.

Finn threw a blanket over himself to cover up the blood, rode up and paid the toll, then crossed over the bridge. The swaying motion caused even more pain. He kept his head down and moaned when the pain became too much. Finally, he was across the bridge.

Five minutes later, he stumbled into a doctor's office and demanded treatment. He brushed aside questions about what had happened, only mumbling something about a hunting accident. Eventually, the doctor had patched him and sewn him up without further questions. He'd lost a lot of blood, the doctor said, and needed rest. Finn fumbled in his pocket for a couple of gold coins and staggered out.

He gathered the reins and dragged himself into the saddle. He stopped for some food at an outdoor market, then took the trail out of town. Now came the hard part. He had to find a place to stay, somewhere near the main trail. He needed to hitch his horse, a distinctive paint, near the trail where Johnny could spot it.

The original plan was for Finn and Red to come south, find a good place to rob, and wait for Johnny Carr. Carr had said that if they found something great, they could pull it off before he got here. They were to meet up in either Waco or Fredericksburg in a town café. If they were in trouble, they should hole up in one of those towns and leave Finn's paint horse some place where Johnny could spot him.

A few hundred yards outside town, he found an old abandoned adobe building. He dismounted and pushed his way inside, turning up his nose at the musty smell.

There was an old, rickety cot in the corner and nothing else. It would have to do.

He tethered his paint in a little homemade shelter somebody had thrown up, open-sided, so the horse could be seen from the trail, hoping nobody would steal it. That's how he'd come by the horse himself. He returned to the shack and the rickety cot. One of three things would happen now. He might get better after resting and having some food and make it back to Robber's Roost. Or Johnny Carr might come through and find him here. Or else he would die here.

He stretched out on the cot and fell into a very light, fitful sleep.

———

Carr was a day or two later than he'd planned on being when he finally left the Roost. His first instinct had been to send Harris and Wood right back out to rustle a few cows on the Santa Fe Trail. Dennison had talked him out of it, reminding Carr they didn't want the Army checking this place out. Carr had to agree with that. He wasn't scared of much, but he didn't need the Army flushing him out of this sweet place he'd found.

Carr struck the trail north to the railroad. First leg was the Atchison, Topeka, and Santa Fe. Railroads, that was the key. That's how they could operate in Texas and hole up in No Man's Land. Finn and Red had a two-day head start on him, but if he pushed it and made the train connections, he could make it to Waco in four days. They might be getting a little itchy waiting for him down there, but that's why it was good to be the boss. He got to give the orders. Carr stuck to his and rode the rails for four hard days.

Finally, he was back on his horse. He reached the edge of Waco after a day on horseback. His horse needed some rest, and he was sleeping in the saddle. He could see the main street ahead of him now, and picked up the pace a little. He needed a saloon and a livery stable for his horse, in that order. A flash of color on his left caught his eye, and he pulled up and turned his horse. The paint tied up outside an old adobe shack looked pretty familiar.

He hesitated on the trail, eyeing the horse and the adobe shack. Finally, wary of a trap, he turned his horse and trotted into town, swinging down from his horse in front of a saloon. Three beers cut the dust from his throat, and he moved down to a café, hoping to see either Finn or Red in the café, as planned.

Carr gulped down a lunch in the café, happy for anything besides the jerky and beans he'd been choking down for the last four days. There was better food to be found when the train stopped sometimes, but he was too busy saving his money. He reminded himself that when he got rich, he planned to hire a chef for the Roost.

Carr finished eating and sat at his table, drumming his fingers on the tabletop and trying to decide what to do next. He decided, as he usually did, that action was better than sitting around and waiting to see what would happen. He dropped some coins on the table, put on his hat, and rode his horse down to the adobe shack.

CHAPTER 4

GENTLEMAN BANDIT

As bad as things had looked when Finn rode into Waco, he knew they were looking worse now. He'd lost track of how many days he had been here. He'd run out of food about twenty-four hours ago, and he was down to his last few swallows of water. Worse, he didn't have the strength to get out of the shack and get what he needed.

Sweat ran down his chest and he propped himself up on the cot, leaning against the back wall. He'd been seeing things today, he was sure of that. He'd started seeing visions of himself with Red, sitting on a pile of gold coins beside a cold mountain stream. Reaching over to lap up some of the water from that stream had caused him to fall out of bed. He almost hadn't had the strength to get back in.

Finn thought he heard steps on the porch outside. Maybe he was imagining that, too. He stared at the door, trying to bring it into focus. He didn't really care who it was out there, if there really was somebody. Things couldn't get much worse.

———

Carr left his horse in a stand of post oak trees fifty yards away from the adobe shack. He moved forward on foot, his hand resting on his Colt as he walked. He had practiced with the Colt a lot out at the Roost. He knew he was good. All he needed was a chance to prove to himself that he was as good with it as he believed.

Stopping beside the paint horse, Carr checked the brand. It was the horse Finn Lonigan had been riding—stolen from settlers headed west on the Santa Fe Trail. Feeling better about the possibility of finding Lonigan inside, he still approached the shack warily. There could be somebody else in there with him.

Carr stepped up to the door and paused to listen. He heard wheezing and some muffled coughs from inside. He turned the knob, opened the door, and stepped inside quickly. The smell of blood and stale sweat was overpowering. Carr fought the urge to gag. Lonigan lay on an old cot and stared blearily at him for several seconds before he recognized his visitor.

"Carr!"

The one word produced a series of short, explosive coughs. Lonigan slid back down to lie flat on the cot.

Johnny Carr crossed the room and sat on Lonigan's saddle, which Finn had somehow dragged into the cabin. He leaned forward, pulled Lonigan's shirt aside, and looked at the wounds. There was a bullet crease across his side that had drawn some blood, but it didn't look too bad.

Carr raised the shirt a little farther and saw a thick bandage high on Lonigan's chest. He moved the bandage, then dropped it back down quickly. This one had bled badly, and it was beginning to smell.

Carr looked around and spotted Lonigan's old Army canteen. He picked it up and shook it quickly. There was a small swallow of water in it. Lonigan held out his hand. Carr gave him the canteen and waited while Lonigan drank what was left in it.

Lonigan held out the empty canteen. "More," he croaked. "I been savin' what was left, just waitin' for you to get here."

Carr stood and turned. "I'll get my canteen," he said. "I'll get you the water, and then we need to talk about what's happened."

Bringing his horse closer to the shack, Carr tied the animal to the limb of a cottonwood tree, taking care to leave him out of sight from the road leading into town. He took the canteen with him.

Carr stepped back into the shack and handed his water to Lonigan. He sat on the saddle again and waited. Lonigan drank greedily, then handed the canteen back. He struggled to sit up, but Carr pushed him back down. He needed Lonigan to have enough strength to tell him what had happened.

Carr waited a moment until the ragged breathing sounded a little steadier. He leaned forward. "Tell me what happened. Where's Red?"

Lonigan's head moved slowly from side to side. "Red done cashed it. Back in a little town near Fredericksburg. Done bought one through the heart."

Carr was fighting down his temper. "How?" he hissed.

Lonigan looked startled for a moment. "We robbed a bank in a little place called Crabapple, near Fredericksburg. Sweet setup. You tole us we could go ahead if we found a good place," he said defensively.

Carr said nothing, but nodded, waiting for more.

"Anyway, this sheriff from somewhere, likely Fredericksburg, was in town. We didn't know about him. He was waiting for us when we come out. Plugged ol' Red with one shot from his pistol, then got me a couple times while I was tryin' to get away. Must have used his rifle on me."

Lonigan lapsed into silence, and Carr realized he was drifting off to sleep. He shook Lonigan's shoulder, causing a gasp of pain. "What about the money?" Carr demanded. "And who has seen you since the robbery?"

Lonigan shook his head back and forth. "We was each carryin' one bag. Red went down with his. I seen it lyin' on the porch of the bank, but I couldn't go after it. I musta dropped mine when I got shot. We didn't come away with nothin'."

Carr fought down an angry growl. "Who has seen you? What about here in Waco?"

Lonigan shook his head again. "Nobody knows me here. I went to see a doc and got patched up a little. Got somethin' for the pain. I stopped an' bought a little food at an outdoor market. Nobody else. Got me a good hideout here."

There was a sound of deep, raspy breathing, and Carr realized Lonigan had drifted off to a tortured sleep. Carr stood and stared down. Lonigan might make it with more help from a doctor, but he couldn't be seen with Lonigan in town. He didn't dare take him to a doctor here in Waco. Harris, back at the Roost, had some medical training from the Army, but Lonigan wouldn't survive that trip.

Carr reached down and picked up an old horse blanket Lonigan had dragged inside. He put it over the muzzle of his Colt, hoping to muffle the sound. He was probably far enough out of town to not be heard, anyway. He aimed the Colt at Lonigan's forehead and pulled the trigger.

Three minutes later, Carr was riding out of Waco, headed for Fredericksburg. He liked the paint horse, but he couldn't take any chances someone would recognize it. He left the horse, along with Lonigan, at the shack. Somebody would get lucky, finding that horse.

———

I walked into the jail bright and early the next morning, hoping things would settle down for good between the Swifts and Hicks. I came from feudin' country myself, and I'd left Kentucky because of it. I knew these things could go on for generations.

The door swung open and shut, and I knew without looking up it was Boone. What I didn't expect, though, was to hear Boone talking all nice and proper, instead of bellerin' something about coffee.

I looked up, and my jaw dropped open when I saw Boone escorting a lady to a chair. He dusted off the chair and hovered over her for a second after she sat, then went and brought her some coffee. I kept on staring, but managed to close my mouth back up.

The lady was maybe in her early fifties, dressed nicely and she was pretty, but lookin' a little flustered. Boone gave her the coffee, then retreated and plopped down in a chair, holding a pencil and some paper. My jaw dropped open again. I'd never seen Boone write down anything, but he was preparin' to write down what this lady said.

I looked over at her again. A little smile played at the corners of her mouth while she watched Boone fussing over her. She was close to twenty years younger than Boone, I figured, and looked like she'd lived a comfortable life. Boone, on the other hand, had been living on gun smoke and beans for almost all his days.

Boone remembered himself in time to look over in my direction. He waved at the lady in the chair. "This here's Miss Alice Brenham," he announced. "She's been robbed by a gentleman bandit."

My jaw dropped again, I'm afraid. "A gentleman bandit?" I finally managed to ask.

"He stuck up a stagecoach and left a poem," Boone told me. He passed over a piece of paper.

I smoothed out the paper on the top of my desk and read the note:

Springtime in Texas

> *It's springtime in Texas, what a day for*
> *a ride*
> *The ladies and gents, all dressed in their best*
> *Roll through the country, with coaches and*
> *horses beside*
> *The gents are hoping the ladies are*
> *impressed*
>
> *Might be a day for a picnic or perhaps some*
> *fine wine*
> *But I'm sorry to tell you, your day's had a*
> *hiccup*

> *You must wait for the day you can enjoy the*
> *sunshine*
> *'Cause today is the day you'll be part of a*
> *stickup*

I looked back up, my eyes going from Boone to Alice Brenham. I confess I probably rolled my eyes a little. "Did this guy actually rob the stagecoach?" I asked.

"He did," Boone thundered. He jumped up to his feet. "Took all the cash money and jewelry from the passengers. Took the strongbox from the coach, too, but the driver said it was empty."

I looked over at the lady. "What did he take from you, ma'am?" I could see I was going to have to take this seriously.

"He took the cash I had with me, which was about fifteen dollars," she said. Her hand went to her throat. "Then he took my mother's pearls. I'm afraid they're the only thing I had left from her."

I looked over at Boone. I had never seen such outrage on his face. Not even the time I drank his beer by mistake over at the saloon.

"Where are the other passengers?" I asked Boone.

"They've gone on to Austin on the stage," he told me. "They told me where they are staying there in Austin for a few days. I'm gonna find this tinhorn and get their money back. And!" he thundered, "I'm going to get Miss Alice's pearls back!"

I was losing the battle not to laugh at Boone. I buried my face in my coffee mug and took a long slurp to steady myself down. "Are you staying in Fredericksburg, then?" I asked Alice Brenham.

Boone answered for her, offering an arm to help her

out of her chair. "I'm gonna check her in over at the hotel," he announced. "Then I'm gonna find this scalawag gentleman bandit and bring him back."

They headed out the door, leaving me chuckling into my coffee mug again. Julia came through the door as they were leaving. She stood aside to let them pass, then came in and asked the obvious question:

"Who was that, and what is going on?"

"I think Boone's in love," I told her.

She stared and waited for me to say something else. I started chortling again.

"Boone's carryin' a torch for that lady. I never saw him act like this before. Not even the times he's had more than his share of beer over at the saloon."

Julia walked over to the window and watched them walking away. "You might be right," she said after they reached the hotel and went inside. "Do you think she likes Boone?"

I shrugged. "Maybe," I allowed. "Some folks just have poor judgment."

That one got me an elbow in the ribs, so I retreated behind my desk and sat down. I told her the story about the gentleman bandit and showed her the note. Julia laughed for a long time, then handed the note back.

"I'm sure Boone will find him," she said. She stood and walked over to help herself to the coffee, then came back and took a seat again. "I actually came over to talk about something serious," she said.

I leaned forward to pay attention.

"It's about Pete," she told me. "He's not happy with working at the ranch, and he and Dad have had several shouting matches about Pete not doing his share, then running off into town here. It's getting ugly. Mom just stays out of it."

She stood and walked over to the window again. "I've talked to Dad and Pete and got them to talk it over a little more calmly. Dad has agreed to give Pete a day off each week, plus one night each week when he can just come to town and do what he wants. He's nineteen now, so he can really do whatever he wants."

She came back and took a seat. "Dad asked me to keep an eye on him now and then to see what he's doing when he comes into town." She pointed down the street. "He usually goes to see that kid that works over at the livery stable. Red hair, kinda big ears, what's his name?"

"Elmer," I said. "Don't know his last name. Just kind of drifted into town one day, got a job at the stables." I frowned. "I think he might have been knocking down some drunks and stealing their money when they come out of the saloon late at night. Haven't been able to prove it, but I think he's trouble."

The crease of worry on her forehead deepened. "That's what I thought, too," she admitted. "He looks like trouble." She reached across the desk and took my hand. "I'm not sure what to do about it," she said. "What do you think?"

I leaned back and stared at the ceiling. "I'll keep an eye on things," I told her. "And I'll keep an eye on Elmer. If I catch him causing problems, I'll toss him in jail for a couple of days and have a talk with Pete myself."

She thought that over, then came around the desk to give me a kiss. "Good," she said. "I'll feel better if you get involved. Just tell me if there's anything more I need to know. I won't say anything to Dad right now."

We agreed to meet at the café for lunch, then she left.

Johnny Carr walked his horse slowly along Jackson Street down to the center of Fredericksburg, then turned right on High Street and followed it down to the mill and the mill race streaming by below it. He dismounted and smiled to himself.

He had counted two banks along his route, and he was pretty sure there must be one or two more nearby. Also, there were several towns in this county, and he'd heard there was just one sheriff and an old deputy to cover it all. It looked like Finn and Red had the right idea, they were just too weak to pull it off properly.

Carr sat down, watching the water rush by, and planned things out in his head. He needed maybe three guys plus a local kid or two to bring him information and hold the horses. He should be able to rob a couple of banks and maybe a big saloon on poker night, plus there was a Texas Ranger armory down the road. It was closed down, but he'd been told there were a lot of guns and ammo in there. Trains were running, too. Maybe they could rob a train.

This was just the boost he needed to turn the Robber's Roost into the fortress he had pictured. His big stone house, a saloon stocked to the gills with anything you'd want, bunkhouses for all his men, and a canyon nearby for all the stolen stock they would drive north to Kansas. He could be a king up there in No Man's Land, with no law to answer to.

The best part about pulling a job in this place was that it wouldn't be in his own backyard. He could pull off the robberies while Dennison kept an eye on things up there, then come home with the money and guns he needed to make things happen. They would just escape on the trains and nobody would be the wiser.

Carr got up and re-mounted. He had passed a telegraph office on his way through town, and it was time to send a message. He reached down and fished around in his saddlebag, finally emerging with a scrap of paper. The name on the paper was Miles Jamison.

Miles had been his sergeant during the war. He was originally from Indiana, but Carr knew he had drifted down to Texarkana after the war was over. He, like Carr, thought there was money to be made in the South. Carr grinned to himself. Both of them had been carpetbaggers before the word was ever invented.

Carr drifted back up High Street until he spotted the telegraph office on his right. He dismounted and tethered his horse, then went inside the office to fetch a pencil and a piece of paper. He sat down on a bench outside, thought for a while, then wrote:

Miles,

   I told you I'd be in touch if I found an opportunity that was worth your while. I've found one. I'm in Fredericksburg and will be here for a few days. Send me an answer and ride this way if you're interested.

Carr
PS Bring a couple more boys with you if you know anybody who'll join us.

Johnny Carr stayed on the bench for a few more minutes, tapping the pencil against his teeth and staring at the note. He decided he was done, took the note inside, and sent it off.

Moving back outside, he mounted up and swung his horse around, looking for the café he had eaten at when he came into town yesterday. Reaching the corner and turning, he stopped about a half block away from the café.

There was a man standing outside the café, shouting at somebody who was apparently inside, eating or getting ready to eat. A crowd gathered around the man who was shouting in the street. He didn't look to be any more than twenty or twenty-one years old.

Carr stopped and listened for a while to what the man was yelling. A grin spread slowly across his face. This was going to be a fight, and Carr loved to watch a good fight. He sat back in the saddle and watched to see what would happen next.

CHAPTER 5

AN OLD FRIEND

I had just settled down with Julia for some lunch in the café when I heard a voice yelling at me from somewhere out in the street.

"McCabe!" McCabe! You wanna take off that badge an' your guns and come out here and back up that big mouth of yours?"

I sighed and looked across the table at Julia. I could see the alarm on her face, but I knew this wasn't something to worry about. "It's Jeb Swift's kid, Zach. He's decided he wants to fight me." I sighed. "I guess that's better than getting himself shot," I mumbled. I got up from the table. "I'll be back in a little while," I told her.

I stepped outside and found Zach Swift out there, along with one of his brothers and a couple guys I'd seen hanging out with Zach at the saloon. Boone had beaten me over here. He was walking around in the crowd, taking money here and there. He came over to me when he saw me step into the street.

"You already been taking bets?" I asked. "I thought you were going after the gentleman bandit."

"I kin wait for a few minutes, can't I?" Boone asked in an injured tone. "Don't hurt a fella to make a couple extra bucks."

I shook my head, then took off my Colt and my badge and handed them to Boone. I turned around to look at Zach Swift.

"You don't have to do this, you know," I told him. "After I whup you, I'm gonna lock you up for causing a ruckus, and your daddy is gonna have to come and get you out of jail. Is that what you want?"

He shook his head and sneered in my direction. "What about after I whip you?" he hissed. "You still gonna lock me up after that?"

I considered that while we circled around each other. "No," I decided. "If you can beat me, I won't lock you up. I wouldn't count on that, though."

He snorted and charged at me, swinging a big right hand. His buddies cheered and waited for him to land that punch. I sidestepped him easily, then gave him a shove as he ran past me, falling into the crowd. I waited while they pushed him back into the circle.

"Not too late, you know," I told him. "You can call this off and go on home. You'll be able to chew your dinner way better if you call it off now."

He hesitated for just a second. He'd expected to land that fist on my jaw and be done with it by now. After a moment, egged on by his buddies, he shook his head and charged at me again.

I easily stepped inside the punch, then swung a hard overhand right to his face. He fell backward into the street and lay there for a minute. His buddies in the crowd stopped yelling. Zach struggled to his feet and put a hand to his nose, which was pouring blood. He stared at me, looking uncertain for the first time.

I shrugged. "We can stop now if you want," I said. "Just take your buddies and go on home."

His pride wouldn't let him back down now. He doubled up his fists again and charged, but he didn't look as sure of himself anymore. I made a move to step inside his punch again, but he held up and screeched to a stop. His right fist sailed past my head and he backed up.

I swung a left uppercut to his belly and heard the air whoosh out of him. He bent over and grabbed his knees. He came up with a handful of dirt, but I'd seen that old trick before. I stepped in and knocked it out of his hand before he could throw it. I backed off and gave him a chance to stop the fight, but then I saw his face twist up with anger. He cursed me and straightened suddenly, throwing a left hook at me. I leaned back and let the punch sail past me, then stepped in with a right hook to his jaw.

My fist connected with his jaw with a solid *crack!* and he fell straight to the ground. He didn't move.

I looked up at his brother and his buddies. "You boys have thirty seconds to clear out of this street or I'll put you in jail along with Zach here. I looked back at his brother. You tell your dad he can come down here and claim Zach at the jail whenever he's ready."

Boone came over, stuffing money into his pockets. "Made thirty dollars," he announced. "Not bad, this bein' short notice and all."

I shook my head and pointed at Zach. "Help me haul him into a cell," I told him, "And then you can go find that gentleman bandit."

Johnny Carr watched with interest as a man wearing the sheriff's badge came out of the café, took off his badge and gun, and walked out into the fight in the street. Something about the sheriff's appearance seemed familiar, and Carr prided himself on his memory. Tall, dark hair, moved around pretty gracefully.

It didn't take long to see who was going to win this fight. The kid didn't have a chance. Lucky for him, the sheriff seemed to be taking it easy on him. Up until the end, anyway. Carr winced a bit when he heard the sheriff's fist connecting with the kid's jaw.

He kept staring while the kid dropped to the ground. The Army...now he had it. Early years of the war, he'd fought with a guy from Kentucky or Tennessee or somewhere. They had both been at Shiloh. They had transferred Carr after that, but he knew this guy. McCabe, that was it. Carr rubbed his hand along his jaw and watched while McCabe and his deputy dragged the kid down the street and into the jail.

When McCabe returned and went back into the café, Carr dismounted, tethered his horse, and went into a saloon across the street. He took a seat by the window and kept an eye on the café to see what else he could learn. He sipped a beer and considered how this might affect his plans. McCabe wasn't the pushover county sheriff he'd hoped for. Certainly not with his fists. Carr would take his chances with his gun if he ever challenged McCabe.

Two beers later, McCabe came out of the café, arm-in-arm with a pretty young lady. Carr watched them go, filing that piece of information away in his brain. So,

McCabe had a girl. That might make him...easier to persuade later on, if that's what was called for.

When McCabe and the girl had gone into the jail, Carr left a coin on the table and crossed the street to the café. He ordered his lunch and considered whether he wanted to go ahead with plans in this county. He ate slowly, turning things over in his head. By the time he'd finished eating, he'd decided it depended on the answer he got from Miles Jamison up in Texarkana.

Good help made all the difference. If he had the help he needed, he would go ahead as planned. If not, it was time to move on. Always play the odds, he reminded himself. Carr left the café to walk around town. Maybe he could find a kid to hold the horses and give him some info on this town, assuming he went ahead with things.

Carr led his horse down to the livery stable. A kid with red hair and big ears came out to help him. Carr talked to the kid for a while. He could use this kid, he knew. Greed always showed, and this kid had greed. Plus, he wasn't too bright. That would help for the jobs Carr had for him. Before leaving, he slipped the kid an extra dollar to take good care of the horse. The kid's eyes lit up.

Carr cut through an empty lot and strolled over to the telegraph office. Much to his surprise, he already had an answer from Miles Jamison. Carr took the message and went outside to read it. He glanced briefly in both directions, leaned up against the wall of the telegraph office, and unfolded the paper. A thin smile crossed his lips as he read:

Johnny,

I've been looking for something like you're talking

about. I'll ride your way. I expect to be there in about
three days. Two of my friends are interested in what
you offer. I'll bring them along.

Miles

Carr folded the paper back up and shoved it into his
shirt pocket. He stayed where he was, leaning up against
the side of the building, while he considered what to do
next. If he was lucky, he could do what he wanted to do
and get back to the Roost before McCabe knew what he
was up to.

The more he thought about that plan, the better he
liked it. If he *accidentally* ran into McCabe and re-intro-
duced himself as an old friend just arrived in town, he
could get McCabe looking the wrong way. Plus, he could
check in from time to time and find out what McCabe
was thinking and planning to do about the robberies Carr
intended to pull off.

Decision made, Carr pushed away from the wall of
the telegraph office and walked back toward the town
jail.

———

Zach Swift had come to by the time I got back to the jail. I
stuck my head around the corner and saw him sitting on
the edge of the bunk, his head between his hands. He
stuck his finger in his mouth and poked it around, probably checking for teeth. He worked his jaw up and down
a few times and touched his swollen nose gingerly.

"Want some water?" I asked.

His head came up, and he jumped a little. He dropped

his eyes to the floor and nodded his head. I poured him a cup of water and gave it to him, then leaned back against the wall while he drank it.

"You called me out in the middle of the town, kid. That didn't leave me much choice. People don't pay much attention to a sheriff who backs down from a fight."

He glanced up, then looked back down at the floor. "Yeah," he said. Several seconds passed. "Sorry," he mumbled.

"Okay." I went back up front and waited for his father Jeb to show up.

An hour passed, and I heard several horses pull up in front of the jail. I looked out the window to see Jeb Swift, the gunhand he'd called Cade, and two more guys I hadn't seen before. They had the look of gunhands too.

Only Swift came inside. The other three dismounted but stayed with the horses outside. Jeb Swift came through the door. He looked surprisingly peaceful to me.

"You got my boy back there?" he asked.

I nodded. "I do." I got up, picked up the keys, and moved around my desk.

"My other boy told me what happened," Jeb volunteered. "Zach's been talkin' big for a while. I warned him about it, but he don't listen to me. You might have done me a favor. Maybe him, too."

I nodded again and walked around to the cells. I opened the door for Zach and stood back. "Your pa's come to get you," I told him.

He didn't look too eager to see his pa. He jammed his hat on his head and walked around the corner.

Jeb knocked the hat off when he cuffed Zach upside his head. "Git out there and git on your horse," he barked. "I'll talk to you later."

Zach left without a word, and I stepped up beside Jeb. I looked out the window. "I see you've still got Cade," I said.

Jeb nodded and said nothing.

"Two new guys, too," I observed. "What are they gonna do for you?"

Jeb shrugged and looked out the window. "I might round up some cows and send 'em up the trail," he mumbled. "I could use 'em for that."

I nodded and kept looking out the window. "I come from Kentucky," I said. "We had a feud goin' on up there. Went on for years. Lot of people died. It's a lot easier to start 'em than to stop 'em, that's what I'm saying."

Swift took off his hat, tossed it around in his hands a few times, then settled it back on his head. "I won't start a range war, Sheriff," he blurted. "If Hicks starts one, I don't plan to lose it, but I won't start it. You have my word on that." He held out his hand.

That took me by surprise. I shook his hand. "Okay," I told him. "Glad to hear it."

I watched as all five of them mounted up and trailed out of town. The trouble was, I thought, that people like Cade and the two new guys don't always do what the ranch boss tells them. Sometimes they just do what they feel like.

———

The jail was empty after the Swifts left, and I didn't have anything to keep me in town tonight. I decided to lock it up and make a quick stop at the saloon before I went home. I was locking up the front door when I started wondering if Boone had found the gentleman bandit.

Julia had told me she was rooting for Boone and the lady who got held up in the stagecoach robbery. Alice Brenham. Boone, Julia told me, had a sweet side to him and she thought he would be kind to the right girl.

I snorted out loud. If Boone had a sweet side, for sure I'd never seen it. I finished locking up and heard a voice I didn't recognize coming from across the street.

"McCabe? Is that you?"

I turned and saw a man crossing the street. Sandy hair, about my age, maybe a couple inches shorter. I watched him come, not knowing who he was. My eyes dropped down and I saw a Union army buckle. That got my attention and gave me a clue. As he got closer, he did look kinda familiar.

"Shiloh," I said emphatically. "You were at Shiloh."

"Sure was!" He finished crossing the street and held out his hand. "Johnny Carr. Company C. Fought right alongside you boys for a couple bad days there."

"They were bad days," I agreed. I had him placed now. I wasn't sure how he'd recognized me so fast, but I remembered him. Hard man to cross, from what I recalled, but a mighty good shot.

We shook. "What brings you to my town?" I asked.

"Business," came the quick reply. "I heard a man can make some money around here, buying cows and sendin' them up the trail to Kansas. You agree with that?"

"A man could do that," I agreed. "Some folks have done real well doing that. I've got some cows myself, but not enough to take any to Kansas."

Carr pointed at the saloon, where I'd been thinking about going, anyway. "Can I buy you some suds?" he asked. "Maybe you can tell me who to talk to and other stuff I might need to know."

I shrugged and turned toward the saloon. "Headed there already," I said. "I'd appreciate a beer."

———

We had a couple beers in the saloon, and I gave him the names of some ranchers in the area, and where he could find them. Carr jotted down the names and asked a few questions about the trail.

The last couple of names I mentioned were Swift and Hicks. "You could talk to both of 'em," I advised him, "but don't let either of them know you're talkin' to the other. It'll turn out better that way."

Carr's eyes probed mine. "Got some trouble?" he asked.

I shrugged, not really planning to say much more.

Carr tucked the paper with the names into his pocket. "I saw some folks ridin' away from the jail when I passed by a couple hours ago," he said. "Looked like a few hard cases in that crowd when they rode by me. Is any of those gents named Swift or Hicks?"

"Old man Swift was one of 'em," I said. "His boy Zach and three hands." I drained the last of my beer. "You could probably call those hands hard cases," I agreed. "I think they'll settle it peaceful, though," I finished. I knew I didn't sound real convincing.

Carr traced his finger in a circle on the tabletop. "You need any help?" he asked. "You got a deputy?"

"I do," I told him. "Good man, too." I hesitated. "He's out of town right now, but he'll be back soon."

He nodded, stood up, and put on his hat. "Good," he said. "If your deputy don't get back in time, or you just need help, I'll be around town for a few days." He leaned down on the tabletop. "Way I see it," he said, "is you and me kinda been through one war together already. You need some help in another, I'll stand by you."

I didn't come up with an answer. He walked away after I nodded. I wasn't a trusting man by nature, and I remembered little about this guy. Still, I reminded myself, Boone was out of town, and I sure didn't want to walk into a shootin' war on one of those ranches by myself. It was something to think about.

I stepped outside the saloon and walked back to the jail. I mounted up on Sherman and took the road out of town. On the way by the livery stable, I saw Carr talking to the livery stable boy. The kid with the red hair, what was his name? Elmer, I reminded myself. I'd promised to keep an eye on him for Julia.

I clucked at Sherman and picked up the pace. I was going to join Julia and her family for dinner. It wouldn't pay to be late.

CHAPTER 6

CHASING THE BANDIT

Pete Hawkins pushed his bay gelding toward town in Fredericksburg, his latest argument with his father still ringing in his ears. His job had been to mend fences on the western edges of the pasture, and he'd done it. The agreement had been he could ride to town on Thursday nights and spend the night in town. His father would never be happy if Pete didn't turn out to love ranching. He didn't, and giving up his free night for more work wasn't going to be part of the deal. More than ever, he was determined to make his own way in the world.

Pete reached the livery stable in time to see his buddy Elmer talking to a man he'd never seen before. He reined in the gelding and watched for a minute, his innate cautiousness taking over. He saw the man reach into his pocket and take out something Pete assumed to be money. He gave the money to Elmer and kept talking.

After a few more minutes, the man turned and walked toward the street. Pete nudged the gelding toward the stable. Elmer waved at Pete, then asked the stranger to stay. Pete rode on in, eyeing the stranger as he dismounted. The man walked over while Elmer made introductions.

Pete gave his name and found out the stranger's name was Johnny Carr. They shook hands. Pete was eager to get on with the evening and impatient for the man to leave.

Elmer clapped a hand on Pete's shoulder. "Johnny has something I can do to make a little extra money," Elmer boasted. "I told him you might be interested, too. Good thing you rode along just now."

Pete was interested, just not as much as Elmer. Still, this might be the start he needed. He nodded slowly, looking at the stranger and waiting.

The stranger turned an easy smile in Pete's direction. "Sure, I've got a couple dollars for you from time to time if you help us out. My men and I are looking to pick up a few cows and some horses for a drive to Kansas. We don't want to make the drive ourselves—we'll hire that out, but we've got to get the herd and horses ready."

Pete nodded, saying nothing. The man shrugged and continued.

"Mostly, we'd just need you to handle the horses. You know, bring along the extras we might buy for a trip. Help us get 'em to the stable for Elmer to watch. You got a day ever' once in a while you could help us?" The easy smile turned up a notch as he waited for Pete's answer.

Pete nodded. He did have one day a week to help, and maybe he could do something with the money. "I got Thursdays off most weeks," he offered. "Mebbe I could help on Thursdays."

The man nodded, seemingly not that interested, but willing to take the help. He glanced over Pete's shoulder and looked at something or somebody behind Pete, who turned to see what the man was looking at.

Instantly, Pete felt anger and knew the blood was rising in his cheeks. His sister Julia was back there, turning her horse just now to ride away. Had Ike sent her to spy on him?

When he turned back, the stranger was turning his attention back to Pete, and the easy smile turned up a couple more notches. He reached out to clap a friendly hand on Pete's shoulder.

"Great," he boomed. "We sure can use your help." He reached into his pocket and came out with a silver dollar, which he pressed into Pete's hand.

"Here's something to make sure you keep your Thursdays open for us," he explained. He shook both their hands and walked back out to the street, waving goodbye to both boys before moving away.

Elmer, clearly excited, waved goodbye. Pete, feeling more confused now than anything else, put the dollar in his pocket, wondering what his sister had been doing out there.

―――――

Johnny Carr walked back toward the saloon, feeling good about the whole evening. He'd renewed his acquaintance with McCabe and offered his help. The kid Elmer was going to handle horses for him. He hadn't really cared about adding on the second kid until he'd seen the girl out there in the street.

That girl was McCabe's girl—he was sure of that. She'd been sitting on her horse out there, watching to see what this kid Pete was doing. Pete had been angry when he saw her, meaning she was probably family, checking up on him. Sister, he would bet.

This got better and better. If he had McCabe's girl's brother holding the horses for a robbery, McCabe's hands were gonna be tied. Carr chuckled under his breath. Finn and Red had been right. This was a sweet setup. They didn't know how sweet. Too bad they weren't gonna be around to see it.

―――――

I'd beaten Julia to the cabin this evening, which was really unusual. Normally she was there waiting for me, even when we went over to have dinner with her family, which was what we planned to do this evening.

When she rode into the yard, something was troubling her, I could see. When she rode in, she gave me a quick kiss, took me by the hand, and pulled me into the cabin. That meant she wanted to talk. I took a seat and waited.

"It's Pete and Dad," she blurted. "Another fight, I followed Pete into town, and I think he's about to get into some trouble."

I waited for more, but she stopped, tears of frustration welling in her eyes. "They fought about Pete's work on the ranch again?" I prompted.

"Yes. Always that." She got up and started pacing. "Pete's never going to love the ranch the way Dad does. Maybe Mom will help him see that eventually. She's at least starting to talk to both of them."

She stopped and sat down, reaching out to take my hands. "Why do you think he's getting into trouble?" I asked.

"That kid Elmer at the livery," she said, "and some other guy I never saw before. I followed Pete into town this afternoon, and I saw some guy at the livery giving money to both Elmer and Pete. What's he paying them for? And who is he?"

"Describe him," I said. "I might know this guy."

Julia shrugged. "I was down the road a bit—not close enough for a good look. But I'd say about your age, maybe a couple of inches shorter, sandy-colored hair."

I nodded. "I think I know who it is," I told her. "Met him in the Army, name is Johnny Carr. I fought alongside his company at Shiloh for a little while. I don't know him very well, but he's here to see about getting a few cows together to run up the trail to Kansas. Maybe he just needs a little help with that, getting together some cows and horses for the drive."

She brightened up a little at that possibility. "Maybe," she agreed. "You know this guy?"

"Not very well," I said, "but he bought me a beer and asked for information about people who might have cows to sell, stuff like that." I paused. "He even offered to help me out if there's trouble with the Swifts and Hicks while Boone is gone."

She looked doubtful again. "Are you going to take him up on that?"

"I don't want to," I admitted. "Boone should be back in a couple of days. It probably won't take him long to sort out this gentleman bandit guy. But if trouble comes up, I'd rather have the help than not."

She nodded, opened her mouth to say something, then stopped.

"Boone should be back pretty soon," I assured her. "He'll come with me if there's trouble. And I'll keep an eye on this thing with Pete and Elmer and Johnny Carr."

She brightened up again and leaned across the table to kiss me. "Okay," she said. "Let's go get some dinner."

————

Boone settled back at his table in the Austin saloon, slurped deeply at his beer, and began to study the maps he'd just been given over at the Risher and Sawyer stage-coach offices. The manager over there had looked him up and down, pretty doubtful about helping. Boone had produced a deputy's badge and talked about the gentleman bandit. That's when he'd gotten the maps.

The gentleman bandit had struck three times now. Only once in Gillespie County, where McCabe was sher-iff, and McCabe had made Boone promise not to start anything outside their county. Boone couldn't really pronounce jurisdiction, but he'd promised McCabe he would only go after the bandit on their turf.

Boone studied the map. The stagecoach had added a loop through Fredericksburg in just the last few years. There was a line that ran from San Antonio to Freder-icksburg and then to Austin. The bandit had struck between Fredericksburg and Austin, when the stage-coach was climbing up a rise and had to slow down. Sounded like the guy had ridden down out of some rocks and had an easy time of it.

Boone studied the map some more, thinking about what he knew about the country that the coach would pass through. That's where he had an advantage—Boone had lived in these parts for over twenty years. There were two places where a robbery would be easy in his county.

One was where the first one had happened. The other was on a stretch of the trail between San Antonio and Fredericksburg.

Boone pushed the map aside, finished his beer, and waved for another. He reached for the schedule they had given him at the stagecoach office. The stage ran every three days. He looked at the calendar on the wall behind him. Tomorrow. That's when the stage would run again. It would run from San Antonio to Fredericksburg tomorrow, stay over and switch horses in Fredericksburg, then run to Austin the next day.

Boone left a coin on the table, picked up the maps and schedule, and walked toward a café, mumbling to himself as he went. He would have to make a guess here —where would this guy strike next? Same place twice, or down south of Fredericksburg the next time?

By the time he'd wolfed down a steak at the café, Boone was ready to bet on the stretch down south, from San Antonio to Fredericksburg. That meant he would have to ride out tonight and sleep under the stars, but he wanted to be ready and waiting for tomorrow. Besides, Boone didn't much like sleeping in a hotel. Under the stars was fine with him. If the gentleman bandit tried again, he would find out that Boone wasn't no gentleman, that's what Boone promised himself.

Boone mounted up and pushed south for a few hours, then cut a little bit east on a trail that would meet up with the stage line trail down below Fredericksburg. Once he'd made enough distance to be sure he could be there and set up early in the morning, Boone stopped and shook out a blanket on the ground. He was asleep almost instantly.

Morning found him sleeping a little later than he'd

expected. The sun was already climbing up when he shook off the blanket. Boone stopped long enough for a little coffee and a hard biscuit he'd packed in his bag before leaving to hook up with the stagecoach trail.

An hour and a half at a brisk pace brought him to a junction with the trail. He joined it and moved south for another half hour until he saw the place, pretty much as he'd remembered it. There was a slow, steady climb up and over a rise in the trail. Scattered oak trees lined both sides—pretty good cover for a bandit there, but it was the nest of boulders at the top that caught Boone's attention.

He moved his horse toward the trees on his right for a little better cover, casting an occasional wary glance to both sides as he climbed the rise. The boulders at the top really had his attention, though. That was a perfect place for a robber to wait.

With another quick glance around him, Boone resumed the climb to the top. A sudden flash of light caught his attention. Had that come from the boulders? Instinctively, he reined his horse sharply toward the trees. A sudden blow on the side of his head knocked him from the saddle. His horse moved on into the trees for another thirty yards, then stopped to graze. Boone lay motionless at the side of the trail.

———

Ike stood, moving along with his cane, as usual, when Julia and I arrived at the big stone house for dinner. He gave me a hug and pushed a beer into my hand, motioning me toward the parlor and the cowhide-covered chairs. I noticed he glanced behind, probably hoping to see Pete, but he said nothing about it when Pete didn't show.

I had a surprise when I came into the parlor. There was another man there, somebody I hadn't seen before. He stood up, and I knew right away this guy had been in the Army. One of the armies, I reminded myself. Folks around here had fought for the Confederacy. This guy stood ramrod-straight and moved toward me, holding out his hand.

Ike made the introductions. "Jake, this here's Leander McNelly. McNelly, Jake McCabe." He waved his arm in a circle and stumped over to sit in a chair.

"Sheriff," McNelly nodded, his voice a deep, pleasant drawl. "Glad to meetcha."

Now I knew where I'd heard that name. McNelly had been a captain in the Texas Rangers, back before they disbanded. Ike had claimed they were getting back together. I wondered what he was doing here.

Ike took over the conversation and talked mostly about cattle and range conditions. He told McNelly about the gentleman bandit and I filled in a few details. Julia came out and joined us for a few minutes. I could see in her eyes the questions she wanted to ask, but we mainly just talked about cows and weather until Julia's mother Jeanne called us in for dinner.

It wasn't until we finished dinner and everybody was pushed back from the table, thinkin' about adjusting our belts, that Ike asked McNelly and me to join him out on the porch. The evening breeze was just kickin' up and we settled down outside. Ike pushed a glass of whiskey into our hands and settled into a chair off to the side.

McNelly glanced at me sideways. "Ike, here tells me you were in the war," he said casually.

"I was," I nodded. "Probly the other side than the one you were on."

McNelly nodded and sipped at his whiskey. "A man does what he needs to do," he observed. "The war's been over for a while now."

I felt some relief. "I got no wish to fight that one all over again," I agreed. "I like it peaceful."

McNelly swung his chair to face me and leaned back. "Tell me what it's like, doin' the sheriffin' around here."

I don't know if it was the beer and whiskey in me, or I just felt like talkin'. I started to tell him about trying to keep a range war about happening down south of here. I told him how some folks weren't too happy I'd fought for the Union, what with me bein' sheriff and all. I told him I didn't trust the Texas State Police, and that was a problem because we didn't have the Rangers anymore.

"All in all," I told him, "I feel like I'm caught in the middle. Between Confederate vets and the Union, between the state police and folks not wanting them involved in things. Just Boone and me to cover the county."

"Caught in the middle," he repeated, nodding his head up and down. "I know just what that feels like. Folks want peace and they want the law enforced. Then somebody tells you how to do it, only they don't know what they're talkin' about." He stopped and stared out across the pasture. "I believe in the law, though," he said softly.

After a minute, he leaned forward and rested his elbows on his knees. "I think you're good people, McCabe," he said abruptly. "I been askin' these questions because the Rangers are getting back together."

I looked past McNelly at Ike, who just nodded his head up and down.

"It's a done deal," McNelly said. "We're getting put back together. I'm going to be captain of a special force, not sure where we're going to be operating yet. I'm tryin' to round up an outfit now."

He stopped and looked across the porch at me. I started shaking my head. "I'm sheriff here for another two years," I said. "I gave my word to these folks—"

McNelly stopped me. "I get it," he said. "You're gonna do what you said. I think that's good. You never know how things will be after a couple of years, though. I think we can help each other, that's what I'm getting at."

I stopped and waited, not sure what he meant.

"You said you don't trust the state police," he reminded me. He didn't wait for me to say anything. "Most folks don't," he agreed. "They're corrupt. What I want is for you to trust the Rangers, to be able to trust me. I think you'll find out my word is good, too."

"That sounds good to me," I said slowly. "What do you need from me?"

McNelly finished off his whiskey and leaned back. "I might need your help sometimes," he said. "I might need you to help me go after somebody in your county. You might be able to give me some information that will help me do my job. I want us to work together."

Julia came out to the porch in time to hear the last part of his little speech, and there was a smile on her face and maybe something else—hope for better times for us. I leaned forward and shook hands. "That's a deal," I told him.

Later on, riding Sherman back to my cabin, I patted

my pocket, where I'd put the name of the telegraph office where I could reach Leander McNelly. It came to me that I might still be caught in the middle of a lot of things, but maybe I didn't have to be alone in the middle.

CHAPTER 7

BOONE

Boone rolled over and his eyelids fluttered open. The sunlight was blinding. He rolled to the side, then clapped a hand to his head and muttered at the pain. His hand came away bloody. His brain tried to process the noise he was hearing. Finally, at the cost of searing pain in his head, he raised up a few inches from the ground, then slumped down with relief. His horse was grazing, just a few feet away. That was at least part of the noise he'd heard.

More sounds came to him, and he laid there, trying to make sense of everything in his mind. Something had hit him in the side of his head while he was riding along the trail. He touched the side of his head again, this time finding the bloody furrow left by a bullet. He grimaced and wiped his fingers off in the grass.

He remembered now. He'd been riding to that nest of boulders up above here to lie in wait for the gentleman bandit. Somebody had bushwhacked him before he got there, that was clear. Why was he still here? They'd been shooting to kill. Maybe he'd been left for dead.

He heard voices now, and he remembered hearing them when he first woke up. Turning slightly so he could see up the trail, Boone was shocked to see a stagecoach pulled over at the side of the road. It wasn't more than thirty yards away. The passengers had been offloaded, and they, along with the driver, were being held at gunpoint while somebody in a mask relieved them of cash and jewelry. The outlaw held a gun on them while they passed a bag between themselves, dropping in their valuables.

Boone looked beside him on the ground, then reached out and pulled his Sharps rifle to his side. He looked over at his horse and saw his shotgun in the scabbard. That was the weapon he needed, considering the shape he was in. His aim didn't figure to be too good right now.

The gentleman bandit, or whatever kind of outlaw he was, was facing away from Boone. Boone had that much going for him. Only the stagecoach driver would be able to see him moving. Slowly and painfully, he began to crawl toward his horse. He made a reassuring clucking noise when the animal shied away from him.

Boone had covered half the distance to his horse when he risked a glance over at the holdup. The robber was still facing away. Boone was pretty sure the driver was tracking his movements from the corner of his eye. The problem, of course, was going to be getting off a shotgun blast with the driver and passengers in the area. A shotgun covered a pretty wide area.

Boone decided to take the problems one at a time. His head was throbbing with pain, and he wasn't sure he'd even be able to get up to his knees to get a shot off. And first, he had to get that shotgun out of the scabbard.

He reached the horse and used his rifle to lever

himself to his knees. He stretched and managed to pull the shotgun free before the horse edged away. He didn't need to check to be sure it was loaded. Before he had left Austin, he'd triple-checked that.

Using the rifle as a brace, he wedged himself around to face the stage. He didn't have much time. The passengers were re-boarding, and the driver was climbing back up top. He stole a glance behind him when he bent to pick up the reins. Boone lifted the shotgun and nodded, then winced again from the pain. The robber was holding a notebook and writing. He tore off a sheet and gave it to the driver.

The robber turned and started back toward his horse. It was now or never. The driver lifted the reins and gave the horses a sharp slap. They leaped forward, and the stagecoach followed with a sharp lurching motion. The robber turned in surprise to see the stagecoach racing away. He swiveled his head to look behind him while Boone raised the shotgun and let go of the rifle he was using for a brace. Boone hoped he would be steady enough to get a shot off.

The robber froze for just a moment, then turned and lifted his rifle. A shot blistered the air above Boone's head. Boone squeezed down on both triggers. The outlaw crumpled to the ground just before Boone passed out and collapsed. The air echoed with the noise of the blasts. Both men lay still on the ground.

———

I stepped out of the sheriff's office on my way to the café for some lunch when I saw the stage from San Antonio rolling into town. As it moved past me, I saw two horses tied off to the back of the stage. One of them was Boone's horse.

The stage rolled to a stop in front of the doc's office and I broke into a trot to catch up with it. The doors opened and Boone came out. He was on his feet, but there were two passengers holding him up. When I got there, Boone was mumbling something about the gentleman bandit and asking about his horse.

I could see a bloody furrow along the side of his head. I hustled into the doctor's office and hurried him outside to help with Boone. We stepped outside just as they boosted Boone up to the porch.

Boone squinted at Dr. Reagan as they walked him inside. "Well," he mumbled. "If it ain't the doc. Probly come to finish me off."

The doc sighed and followed Boone into the office. "I'll take care of him," he promised me, "but it doesn't sound like there's anything wrong with his head that wasn't wrong before."

The doors swung shut, and feeling a little relieved, I moved back over to the stagecoach. The driver was moving among the passengers. A couple of them had some blood on them, but I had a feeling it was Boone's blood.

I nodded at the driver, and he came over to talk to me. He handed me a piece of paper and told me a high-wayman had tried to rob them. The robber wrote the note, he explained.

A quick glance told me this was a poem. "Where's the bandit?" was my first question.

The driver pointed back down the trail out of town. "Boone killed him with his shotgun," he answered. "I threw a couple blankets over him to keep the buzzards away, but I ain't done nuthin' else with him. I figgered you might want to have a look before he gets buried. I've got his horse tied to the back of the stage, there."

A door opened at the hotel three doors down, and a lady moved down the street toward us. After a moment, I could see it was the passenger from a few days ago, Alice Brenham. "Is it Billy?" she asked, grabbing at my sleeve.

"Billy?" I stared at her blankly.

"Mr. Boone. Billy Boone. Was he hurt?"

"Oh," I said. "Boone. A bullet grazed the side of his head. Doc's looking at him now."

She turned and headed for the doctor's office. I trailed along behind her. She opened the door, and Boone's voice filled the hallway.

"You ain't keeping me in here, you old sawbones, you. You'll probly try to charge me fifty cents a day for this bed. I can sleep better over at the livery. You probly got some horse pills you'll try to feed me. You..."

Boone's voice trailed away and died when he saw Alice Brenham. She hurried over to his side.

"Now, Billy," she scolded him. "You have to do what the doctor says to get well." Her fingers moved to the side of his head, and she gasped when she saw the furrow in his skull. "You lay down," she commanded, "and do what the doctor says."

Boone's mouth opened and closed a couple times, but no words came out. Finally, he just laid back on the bed, rolling his eyes in my direction.

"Well, I never," Dr. Reagan breathed. He looked over at Alice Brenham. "Must be an angel, sent from heaven above." He decided. "Only thing I've ever seen that could stop Boone from griping."

Boone glared in the doc's direction, but he still didn't have any words.

I decided to press my luck. "That's right, Billy," I said. "You do what the nice lady says and mind the doc here." I escaped out the door before he could start cussin' me.

Outside, I found the driver had polled the passengers, and they all wanted to continue on into Austin first thing in the morning. None of them were wounded. The driver pointed them toward the café and told them the stage would leave at first light. I told the driver I would find the spot where the bandit had struck and bury him.

I led Boone's horse and the bandit's horse over to the livery and left them there. Before I left the livery, I took the saddlebag from the bandit's horse and also searched his saddle for anything else I could find. There was nothing besides the saddlebag. I took that with me back to the sheriff's office.

I left the saddlebag beside the desk and opened the paper the driver had given me. I smoothed it out and read the note inside.

> *There's blue skies above and bluebells below*
> *It's really quite purty around us, you know*
> *Time to think about thangs you like the best*
> *Hang on to those, let go of the rest*
>
> *Money and jewels, they'll catch your eye*
> *But you got to stop and ask why*
> *You can't take 'em with you, they'll stay here*
> *   below*
> *So pass 'em to me, and off I will go*

I snorted out loud and laid the note down. He'd

written his last poem, and it was a good thing for more than one reason. My school teacher would have slapped my hands with a ruler if I'd turned that one in.

I picked up the saddlebags and shook out what was inside onto the desktop. There was a lot of money, some rings and watches, and a pearl necklace. I set the necklace aside. I could reunite that with its owner. The rest, I decided, I would take to the stagecoach offices in Austin and let them sort it out.

I stood, threw the saddlebag over my shoulder, and picked up the pearl necklace. I stopped off at the hitching rack outside the office and tossed the saddlebags over Sherman, then continued on down to the doc's office.

When I opened the door and went in, the doc was in his office with another patient, and Boone was lying down on his cot outside. Alice Brenham was sponging off his wound with a clean rag and a pitcher of water. Boone glared at me.

I gave the necklace to Alice, and she thanked me. Boone picked up the water glass on the table beside the cot and asked her if she would get him some water. She took the glass and left the room, and Boone pointed his finger at me.

"You call me Billy again, or tell anybody else my name is Billy, you're a dead man," he growled.

"Sure, Boone," I said. "I'll just go back to calling you Boone, like always." He laid back on the cot and looked satisfied. "I was just wonderin', that's all," I said over my shoulder as I left.

"Wonderin' what?" he asked, his voice full of suspicion.

"Just wonderin' if your mama knows you don't use the name she gave you," I said. He came up halfway off the cot and I made my escape out the door. I had to admit I was enjoying this more than I should have.

I grabbed the posters I had in my office just to see if anybody's face matched the dead man Boone had shot. I followed the stagecoach's trail south, out of town, and came to the holdup spot about an hour later.

I worked my way to the top of the rise through the trees. There was nobody up there. I came back down and saw where the corpse lay, there beside the trail. I pulled up the blanket and went through my posters, but this guy wasn't one of them.

I pulled out a shovel I had brought with me and started digging. I buried the robber right where he had fallen.

I rode back to Fredericksburg, leaving the money and jewels at the stagecoach office and filling out some paper-work for them. The saddlebags I kept with me, and made it over to the café in time for a late dinner.

I thought about checking in on Boone but decided to leave well enough alone. Besides, I reminded myself, he didn't want to see me. The man was in love.

———

Johnny Carr stepped into the Scholz Garten saloon in Austin and stopped for a second, letting his eyes adjust to the smoke and darkness. He squinted at a guy stepping away from the bar and moving in his direction. This guy was heavier than before and wasn't sporting as much hair as he used to, but it was Miles Jamison, the man he'd come to meet.

Carr shook hands quickly, not wanting to call any

attention to himself, and followed as Jamison led the way to a table in the corner.

Carr had decided to meet them in Austin because Fredericksburg was smaller and he didn't want them noticed around town. Specifically, he didn't want them noticed by McCabe. That guy didn't seem to miss much. Carr knew he couldn't keep these boys off the streets and out of sight for very long. He didn't mind if anybody spotted them in Austin. He couldn't afford to be noticed in Fredericksburg. Carr would only make this one trip and meet them just once.

Jamison made the introductions, but Carr didn't really care about names. One had light blonde hair, the other had a very long beard. Carr would remember them as Blondie and Beard. They looked like they could handle themselves in a fight. That's all he cared about.

Carr gave them his speech. Even Jamison didn't know about most of this.

"I've got the best hideout you've ever seen," he started. "Up in No Man's Land. You know about that? North of Texas, between the Nation and New Mexico?"

He got a couple of nods and kept going. "Got me a big rock house, gonna build me some bunkhouses and cabins for my boys. There are settlers coming down the Santa Fe Trail and we can take their money and cattle. We can take cattle and money in New Mexico too, plus we can raid down here in Texas. An' the best part is, there's no law in No Man's Land." He looked around. "And I'm gonna put in the best saloon you've ever seen."

"Women?" asked Jamison.

"Maybe," was his answer. He didn't plan on bringing in women. That would start trouble and fights, sure as he was sitting here. No point in telling them about that now, though.

"What I need now," he continued, "is more money, guns, and ammunition. I got the first job lined up—a bank in a place called Kerrville. Sleepy town, lots of German farmers, looks like a lot of money in the bank. I can tell you the rest later."

Carr stopped while a server set down another pitcher of beer. He looked around the table. "You do this, I'm the boss, we do this my way. Good money for everybody. You all in on this?"

First, he got a nod from Jamison, then Blondie, then Beard.

"Good," Carr said as he reached for the pitcher. He poured a glass for everybody, then told them more about the bank in Kerrville.

———

Mornings were my favorite time to be sheriff. If I'd had to throw anybody in jail the night before, I could generally let them out in the morning. Then it was pretty quiet around town for a few hours. Sometimes Julia came into town with breakfast and coffee. Those were my favorite days.

This morning, I had started out by going to the café and getting some breakfast for Boone. I took it into the doctor's office as a peace offering. He looked a little suspicious, but when I didn't call him Billy, he calmed down. Alice Brenham came in early to look after him, and I came back down to the office.

Things were quiet for over an hour, but my first visitor was a surprise. I heard the door open and shut, then looked up to see Zach Swift in my doorway. He was holding his hat with both hands, and he waited to be invited in. He had some purple bruises on his face.

I waved at the chair next to my desk. "What brings you to town, Zach?" I asked.

He moved over to the chair, but didn't sit down. "There's trouble," he blurted. "Out at the Hicks place. That guy Cade and the other two gun hands, they've gone to cause trouble and take the cows."

"How do you know?" I asked, coming out of my chair. "And where's your dad?"

"I was in the back of the barn forking out some hay. I heard them talking, but they didn't know I was there. They've been looking for a herd to steal and take up the trail. They don't care who they shoot."

Zach broke off talking, watching me while I buckled on my Colt and picked up my Winchester.

"Where's your dad?" I asked.

He waved his hand at the street. "He came to town this morning. That's all I know. I looked for him a little, but then figgered I needed to tell you."

I patted him on the shoulder on the way by. "Thanks, Zach," I told him. "You did the right thing. Keep looking for your dad. Tell him I need him out at the Hicks place."

I trotted outside, shoved the Winchester in the scabbard, and put one foot in the stirrup. A voice from behind me stopped me.

"You look like you've got some troubles," the voice said. "Need a little help?"

I half-turned to see Johnny Carr standing there. I stayed where I was, halfway in the saddle. Boone couldn't help, he was down for several days. I stared at Carr, trying to make up my mind.

CHAPTER 8

WATER WARS

I pulled my foot back from the stirrup and turned to face Carr. Things weren't in my favor, the way it stood right now. Cade, plus two more gunhands, and they had likely taken the Hicks family by surprise. Maybe it was good luck that Carr showed up just now. Part of me wondered if that was too good to be true. Carr just stood there, looking a little puzzled when I didn't answer.

Decision time. I took a deep breath and nodded. "Could be that range war I was talking about," I told him. "You sure you want a part of this?"

Carr checked his Colt and Henry rifle, turned around, and mounted up. "Like I told you before," he said. "We went through one war together. I'll back you on this one."

I mounted and turned Sherman to go, but another question from Carr stopped me.

"Badge?" he asked. "Am I going in as a deputy?"

A little voice inside me said I shouldn't give him a badge. I wasn't sure why that thought popped up. I had several deputy badges in my desk, but I shook my head.

"Consider yourself a deputy," I told him. "We'll worry about the badge if we need it later."

Carr shrugged and pulled up to ride beside me as we left town.

A few miles passed in silence while I tried to figure out what to do. It really depended on the state of things when we got to the Hicks ranch. If the shooting hadn't started, maybe I could still settle things down. It would help me to have Carr holding a gun to back me up.

If the shooting had started, I would have to come in on the side of the Hicks. It was, after all, Swift's hands who were riding out to cause trouble. Hicks's son Caleb could make everything worse, though. He was itchin' to put a notch on that gun of his.

Carr's words interrupted my thoughts. "What're you figgerin' to do when we get there?" he asked.

Reasonable question. I didn't have a good answer. "If the Swift boys—a gunman named Cade and two others—if they're already shootin', then we take them down. Don't make a target of yourself, but if the shootin' war has started, we stop this now."

One other thought struck me a minute later. "We take prisoners if we can. Don't put yourself out there as a target, but don't take a bullet without shootin' back. If you don't have to, don't shoot anyone. If you're getting shot at, fire away. Let the judge sort it out when he comes through town."

Carr only nodded. I wasn't sure what that meant. We rode on for another mile, and then I heard what I was afraid I'd hear. There were gunshots—lots of them— coming from the Hicks ranch house, just over the rise.

We crested the hill and looked down. The corral fences around the barn were mostly lying on the ground.

Cattle were milling around beyond the house. Thick dust hung in the air. It looked like they had driven a stampede by the barn and house to get close. Now the Swift gunfighters were out by the barn, barricaded behind woodpiles, or what was left of the fence, or hidden behind the corners of the barn.

One man was down in the yard between the barn and the house. I took it to be one of Hicks's hands, lying on the ground at a funny angle. He wasn't moving. I figured the stampede had trampled him.

We watched for a minute. There was some gunfire comin' from the house, but maybe only two guns, I figured. The Swift hands had the house bracketed. I could see movement from the side of the barn closest to me. I moved sideways and put my field glasses on the movement. Somebody was down and bleeding. It looked like the younger Hicks boy, Caleb. One gunman was standing near him, holding him down with his boot and firing at the house. More gunfire came from the center area of the barn and the far side.

Carr moved up next to me. "Your call," he said. "Want me to go around the barn?"

I lowered the field glasses and nodded. "You take that side, I'll take this side. The Hicks don't know you," I cautioned. "Don't make yourself a target for them, either. Everybody's likely to shoot at you." I glanced over and stopped when I saw his face. He was excited. I could have understood nervous, or scared, or on edge. This was excitement, and that troubled me. Nothing I could do about it now, but it was something to remember.

I scratched out the lay of the land with a stick on the ground and sent him on his way, looping around to the far side of the barn.

Moving back down the slope a bit, I hobbled Sherman, took my Winchester out of the scabbard, and moved back over the top of the rise and started down the slope. I stayed low and cut back and forth, but I was pretty sure the Hicks would know my hat, would know it was me. I moved steadily down toward the barn. The Swift gunman on this side was entirely concentrated on the house in front of him and the wounded kid he had pinned to the ground.

When I was fifty yards away, I dropped to my belly and crawled another twenty-five yards. I came up to my knees and lifted the Winchester. Caleb Hicks saw me and stopped his struggling, dropping straight to the ground.

"Hey!"

My shout took him completely by surprise. He spun and lifted his rifle. I shot him cleanly through the chest, and another shot from the house turned him sideways as he fell. I covered the remaining ground in a crouching run. The guy I'd shot was down for good. It wasn't Cade, but I knew it was one of Swift's other gunfighters. Caleb Hicks had taken a shot through the leg earlier, his eyes were bright with the pain.

Gunfire was coming from the center of the barn, around a slight corner but close to me. "Hang in there kid," I said. "I'll be back."

Caleb gritted his teeth and nodded. I edged around the corner and saw a patch of somebody's red shirt. Whoever he was, he was firing at the house. I lifted my Winchester again, holding a little left of the red patch.

When I fired, there was a yelp of pain, then a rifle clattered to the ground. Somebody dashed into the barn, chased by several shots from the house. I raised my Winchester and waved it toward the house. I needed them to understand I was going in, and they needed to stop firing. After a moment, the gunfire stopped.

I edged to the barn door, then stopped to listen. I couldn't hear anybody moving around in there. Going through that front door sounded like suicide to me. He was going to be waiting for me, like the main prize in a turkey shoot.

I crawled back to Caleb. "Is there another way in?" I asked.

He nodded and pointed to his right. "My brother Adam and I were fighting a couple years ago," he said through gritted teeth. "He threw me into the barn and cracked a few boards. You can probly crawl through."

I patted his shoulder and left him with my Winchester. "If that guy comes out, you know what to do," I said.

I crouched down and moved quietly down the length of the barn, looking for the cracked boards. Near the back, I found them. I laid down flat and peered inside. There was light streaming through in places, coming from the cracks between boards. I could see it was Cade in there, watching the door. He was standing, Colt in hand, waiting for me to come through.

I laid out flat on the ground, keeping my Colt in my right hand as I wormed my way slowly into the barn. I fought the urge to sneeze, with the hay pushing into my face and the dust coming from the floor. Foot by foot, I made my way in, then rose to my feet.

"Cade," I said.

He turned his head slowly, still holding the Colt. He saw I had the drop on him and slowly pointed the gun in the air and turned to face me. There was blood on his left sleeve, but he was standing steady, and those eyes never left my face. His gun moved slowly until the barrel was at the side of his head.

"You've got the drop," he admitted. His gaze traveled down to my Colt. "I think I could take you, Sheriff," he murmured. "Anyways, you're not taking me in alive. I been to prison before. Have you got the sand to give a man a fair chance?"

I stared at him for several seconds, then nodded. He holstered his Colt and waited. Slowly, I dropped my gun back in the holster and returned his gaze. I was watching his eyes.

When those eyes flickered, I drew the Colt in one long, steady move. He dropped down a little and moved to the right. My first shot struck him in the left shoulder and he spun, firing a harmless shot into the wall of the barn. My second shot hit him dead center. He pitched over onto his back. I came up to him slowly, keeping him covered. When I reached him, his eyes were glazed over.

I left him there and came out of the barn the way I'd come in. I didn't need no happy trigger fingers out there. The Hicks, old Zeke and his wife, had reached Caleb. His mother was pressing a rag to his leg to stop the bleeding. Adam, the older boy, was standing in front of the house, still holding his rifle and looking past the far side of the barn.

Zeke stood as I walked over. "Got to get some water," he said to his wife. Seeing me, he pointed toward the far side of the barn. "Your man got the drop on the other one," he said. "Got him covered."

As soon as he spoke, there were two gunshots from the far side of the barn. Adam Hicks, still standing in front of the house, stayed where he was. I ran to the corner of the barn, Colt up and ready. "Carr!" I shouted.

"Here," came a quick answer.

I rounded the corner and found Johnny Carr standing over the third Swift gunman. He was down, shot through the heart.

"He made a move on me," Carr explained. "I had to shoot him."

I slowly holstered my Colt and dragged my sleeve across my face to wipe the sweat away. "Okay," I said. "We're done here."

Hoofbeats sounded in the yard, and I hustled back to the front. Old man Jeb Swift and his son Zach were sitting on their horses, hands in the air. Zeke Hicks held a shotgun on them.

"Easy," I said to Hicks, slowly pushing the barrel of the shotgun down. "Jeb didn't start this war. His hands started it while he was gone. He didn't know."

————

Half an hour later, Caleb Hicks was in the back of a buggy, on his way to town. His mother was taking him to see Doc Reagan in Fredericksburg. I had made Zeke Hicks and Jeb Swift sit down on the porch and talk things out. After a little shouting and a lot of finger-pointing, they shook hands, and the Swifts left.

Johnny Carr went out to load the dead men on their horses so I could take them back to town. I stood to leave and stepped down off the porch. Adam Hicks, Zeke's oldest boy, came out and walked to my horse with me.

"Sheriff," he said. "That guy you brought here with you—he had Swift's man covered. He didn't have to shoot."

I stared at him. "What did you see?" I asked.

"Your guy had him covered with his rifle. Swift's guy had his hands in the air. Your guy put his rifle down, backed up, and challenged him. Cussed him, called him names. I could hear it. Egged him into haulin' that smokewagon. Soon as the guy reached for his gun, your man pulled iron and shot him. I seen it all."

I patted my horse's shoulder absently and looked at Adam. I didn't have any reason to think he was lyin' to me. Johnny Carr was tying the last of the attackers over his saddle when I looked at him.

"Thanks, Adam," I mumbled. "I believe you." I looked over at Carr one more time. "Let's just keep this between us for now."

———

I dropped off the bodies at the barbershop. Vince, the barber, was getting so much burial business these days he was either gonna have to give up the barberin' or the burying folks.

Johnny Carr was still mounted when I came out. I went over to thank him for backing me up.

"I had to shoot him, ya know," he snapped. I hadn't said anything about it, so it seemed pretty strange to me he said that, coming out of nowhere.

I just nodded and thanked him again. He tipped his hat and rode off. I turned and saw Julia at the door to the doctor's office. I'd completely forgotten we had planned on dinner in town at the café. I wondered if she had seen me bringing in the dead guys. Her eyes lingered on the barbershop as I walked up, so I had my answer.

I gave her a hug and a kiss. She kissed me, but then held me at arm's length, searching my face.

"Shootin' war out at the Hicks place," I said. "I had to ride out and stop it. Jeb Swift's hands were really more like gunhands than cow hands. They didn't want to come in peaceful. I'm fine," I added.

She gave me another hug and looked past me at the barbershop. "Are the dead men all Jeb Swift's hands?" She pointed behind her at the doc's office. "They brought Caleb Hicks in here a while ago. He'll be fine."

"All of 'em were Jeb Swift's hands," I answered. "He didn't want the fight—they did it on their own."

She took my arm and turned me toward the doc's office. "Boone wants to see you," she said. Then, after a pause: "Did you shoot all three?"

"No, two of 'em, I did. Johnny Carr, the new guy in town I told you about, he came to help me and he shot the other one."

We moved inside and sat by Boone's cot. Alice Brenham was still there. I grinned a little to myself at that. They wanted to know more about the shootout and I explained what had happened. At the end, when Alice had left for the evening, I told Julia and Boone what Adam Hicks had told me about Carr shooting down the last gunman.

They both looked at me, pretty much at a loss for words, it seemed to me. Boone cleared his throat and laid back on the cot.

"Well," he said. "At least this Carr guy helped you." He stopped and reached for a drink of water. "I wouldn't trust him next time," he added.

We all agreed on that one. Boone said he would be there for me the next time, and I was glad, not for the first time, to have him in my corner.

Julia and I said our goodnights to Boone and headed down to the café.

————

Johnny Carr was grinning to himself as he rode out of Fredericksburg. This, he thought, couldn't have gone better. He had pulled the sheriff's fat out of the fire and made himself into an upright citizen in Fredericksburg. People had waved and tipped their hats to him this morning.

The thrill of taking down that gunman this morning had been unbelievable. He had killed men during the war, but it was nothing like this. If he was going to be really hard on himself, he had to admit he might have drawn before the other guy was completely ready. Still, he'd won with ease. The other guy barely got a shot off.

There was something bothering him at the back of his mind. Carr frowned for a moment and tried to remember what that was. Now it came back to him. McCabe might be a little suspicious about what happened out there when he shot the guy down. That made the day a little less perfect.

Plus, from what they had told him, McCabe had crawled into that barn with only his Colt. He'd come out without a scratch, and Cade, a known gunhand, was dead. That brought a frown to Carr's face. Maybe McCabe was better with a gun than he thought. Still, he reasoned, McCabe might have cheated a little, too. Nobody else had been in that barn to see what happened.

Carr was about to reach the meeting spot he had set up with Jamison, who had told him he might have a recruit to join the gang. Carr wasn't eager to trust somebody new, but he might have a job for the guy.

He pulled up and dismounted in the shadow of a cottonwood tree. Jamison was standing there with a guy who carried some extra pounds, Carr observed. He walked over for the introductions. Jamison introduced the guy as Wagon.

Carr stared at the new guy. "Wagon?" he asked.

Wagon shrugged. "I just come off a trail drive to Kansas. They said I hung around the chuck wagon more'n most."

Jamison chuckled. Carr's grin faded almost immediately, replaced by a hard stare. "Jamison told you what we're gonna do?"

Wagon nodded. "You're ready to do your share?" Carr asked.

Wagon nodded again.

"Okay, I've got a job for you," Carr said at length. "Not what you think, though. I need you to go north and get a couple more of my men."

Wagon hesitated, looking confused, then simply said, "Okay, whatever you want."

Satisfied, Carr reached into his pocket, pulled out a few gold coins, and handed them over. "You take the train from Austin to Dallas," he said. "You've got to move fast. In Dallas, you switch the KATY—Missouri, Kansas, and Texas railroad. You take that to Topeka, then switch to the Atchison, Topeka, and Santa Fe. Take that to the end of the line in Kansas. Then you ride to my hideout in No Man's Land."

Carr stopped, pulled paper and a pencil from this saddlebag, and drew a map. "This is how you get there when you get off the last train," he said. He stopped while Wagon studied the map, then nodded.

"Trains are the key to this operation," he said, locking in on Wagon's eyes. "We stay ahead of everybody else—that's how we can work Texas from No Man's Land. You get that?"

Carr waited, studying Wagon's face for several seconds. Satisfied, he handed over the map.

"When you get there, you tell Dennison he stays there, and Harris and Wood come with you to meet up with us. Get back to Waco the fastest way you can. Come by train as far as you can, just the way you went up. You get to Waco, you stop. One of you goes to the Main Street Café every morning until you see me there. Only one of you at a time. Clear? You got it? I'm giving you ten days to get there and bring my guys back. No more."

Carr held his eyes while Wagon shuffled his feet uncomfortably, cleared his throat, and finally said, "Got it." When Carr kept staring at him, he turned, mounted his horse, and rode off toward Austin.

Johnny Carr watched him go, and he was feeling better about things again. McCabe might be suspicious, and he was a pretty salty customer, but Carr was going to have the numbers. There were a lot of banks between here and No Man's Land.

CHAPTER 9

TROUBLE IN KERRVILLE

Pete Hawkins saddled up and rode out early on his day off. Today was the first day he would start to make some of his own money, start to live his own life. He had already decided he would move away from the ranch. Maybe he would move to Fredericksburg, maybe all the way to Austin. Either way, he was going to earn two dollars today by gathering some horses and cattle for Johnny Carr. It was a start.

Cantering down the trail to Fredericksburg, he arrived in town and moved toward the livery stable, where he was to meet with Elmer and Johnny Carr and find out a little more about what he would do today.

He arrived to see Johnny Carr handing some coins to Elmer and mounting his horse. Pete arrived at the livery just as Carr was leaving. Carr just nodded and pointed back at Elmer. "He'll fill you in," Carr told him. "I'll see you pretty soon."

Pete turned to watch him go, feeling he had been ignored. The day hadn't even started yet and Carr had already left. Elmer waved him in and handed him two one-dollar coins. "For today's work," he explained. "Paid it all in advance. I don't get paid at the livery until I've already worked a whole week."

Pete nodded and stuffed the money in his pocket, feeling a little resentful. He couldn't be sure how much money Carr had given Elmer, but he had the feeling that Elmer had more coins in his pocket than Pete.

Elmer turned toward the livery. "I've got a couple horses to feed here before we go," Elmer explained. "You can help me out or not, suit yourself."

Pete shrugged, dismounted, and helped Elmer with his chores at the livery. When he asked about what they would do that day, Elmer just shrugged and said they would buy some cattle and horses from German farmers near Kerrville, then drive them back to where Carr was holding the cattle.

Twenty minutes later they left the stable, moving through Fredericksburg and striking the trail south-west toward Kerrville. Pete held a hand to his hat all the way through town, covering his face. He wasn't sure why he did that, but it had something to do with a little nervousness he was starting to feel about this job.

A few miles out of town, Pete could see some horsemen pulled over at the side of the road. He counted four men, and as they drew closer, he could see one of them was Johnny Carr. Carr waved and motioned for them to pull up alongside.

Pete was introduced to the other three men. He got the names Jamison, Blondie, and Beard. All of them had their hats pulled low and had bandanas under their chins. It seemed like a lot of men to buy cows and horses, and Pete wondered why Carr needed him. They left and rode single-file down the trail, with Pete and Elmer bringing up the rear.

The group passed several herds along the way, and Pete expected to pull in several times to buy animals, but they kept going. When they began to pass a few scattered buildings along the trail, he knew they were in Kerrville.

When the group left the trail and pulled into a dusty field next to one of the buildings, Pete squinted to read the name on the front of the building. "CNB Bank of Texas," he murmured to himself. The group dismounted around him and two of them handed their reins to Pete. The other two handed their reins to Elmer, who Pete now noticed was directly behind Pete, blocking his road out.

Pete stared at the empty hitching rail in front of the bank and looked over at Carr, who just shrugged. "It might get crowded," he explained. "We'll leave the hitching rail to other folks." He gave Pete a hard stare, then the four walked toward the bank.

Pete held the reins he'd been given, feeling worse by the minute. It dawned on him he didn't really know any of these men. Elmer had met Carr and introduced them, but the others he'd seen for the first time today. Pete took comfort for a moment by remembering that his friend Elmer was with him.

It was silent for a few minutes, then two shocking things happened at once. First, an elderly gentleman walked up to the bank and opened the front door. Almost immediately, he turned and tripped, falling face down in the dirt. He stayed there, hands over his head.

Instantly after that, a gunshot rang out from inside the bank. Knowing now what was happening, Pete turned his horse to run. The first thing he saw when he turned was Elmer's gun, which had been shoved into his belly.

"You stay here and wait for 'em," Elmer snarled. "You try to run, you'll take a bullet in the belly. Carr's orders."

Elmer's face curled into a cruel smile. Pete got the feeling his *friend* Elmer was prepared to do just what he said.

Another gunshot sounded inside the bank, then Carr and the three others burst out the front door, bandanas over their faces. Carr and Jamison both carried gunny sacks. The elderly man on the ground hadn't moved. Pete didn't know if he'd been shot or he was just too scared to move.

The four men ran toward the horses. Pete watched them, feeling like time had slowed down to a crawl. He couldn't leave without being gut-shot by Elmer. A man ran out of the bank and fired a shot at them. Carr turned and returned the fire. The bank employee staggered backward and slid down the wall. The gun fell from his hand.

The reins for the two horses were yanked from his hand and everyone mounted around him. Someone else ran out of the bank, then dove inside immediately when Carr and his men fired.

Pete found himself in the middle of the group, leaving town at a thundering gallop. He had no choice but to move with them. Besides, people were shooting at them back there at the bank.

They kept up the blistering pace for a few miles until Carr, in the front, held up his hand to slow it down. He pulled down his bandana and the others did the same. They moved on at a trot. Pete noticed he was still surrounded by the others.

Pete's brain couldn't seem to sort through what had happened this morning. He had started out to hold some horses and gather some cows. Now, he had been part of a bank robbery.

A mile outside of Fredericksburg, Carr called a halt and motioned for the others to gather around him. He addressed Jamison, Blondie, and Beard first, telling them to go back to their cabin. He would join them later and split the money, he told them.

Next, Carr dismissed Elmer, telling him to go on back to the livery stable. If anybody asked where he'd been that morning, Elmer would tell them he had been sick and got to work late. Carr passed some money to Elmer before he left.

Pete watched while Elmer rode away, then turned to face Carr, who rode up close and leaned into his face.

"You're part of us now, kid," he said. "You were part of a bank robbery this morning."

Pete started to shake his head back and forth. Carr pulled off a glove and slapped Pete across the face.

"You're part of us," he repeated. "Let me explain what's going to happen if you try to quit us or think about telling anybody about this morning."

Carr leaned in even closer. Pete would remember the smell of whiskey breath and stale cigarette smoke for a long time.

"I won't kill you first," Carr hissed. "I'll go after your family first. Your old man on the cane, your Ma, and your brother. I'll save your sister for last, but she'll die too. And I'll tell her boyfriend that you're a bank robber."

Carr stopped to let what he had said sink in. He held Pete's eyes with a blistering stare. "Do you want any of this to happen, kid?"

Pete shook his head back and forth numbly.

"Can't hear you, kid," Carr snarled.

"No," Pete mumbled, "I don't want any of that to happen."

"Good," Carr said, sounding satisfied. He held out three silver coins. "Here's something extra for today."

Pete started to shake his head no, then he caught the look on Carr's face. He reached out, took the coins, and mumbled, "Thank you."

Carr nodded and pointed down the trail, telling Pete he could go on home. Pete rode down the trail for a few minutes, feeling like he was in a bad dream. When he rounded a corner on the trail and could no longer see Carr, he dismounted, stepped over to the side of the trail, and vomited.

———

Julia was doing her least favorite job. She hung a rug over a tree limb outside the back door and started beating it with the broom. Clouds of dust billowed out, as always. She adjusted the bandana over her mouth, then the one over her hair, and started beating again. Where did all the dust in Texas come from?

She heard hoofbeats and turned around to see Pete trotting his horse into the corral. He unsaddled and turned the animal loose, then rushed past Julia into the house. He was noticeably pale. Julia turned and looked at Pete's horse, which was lathered up and tossing his head, circling the corral.

She turned and trotted into the house. Pete had gone to the room he shared with his brother and shut the door. A drawer slammed loudly inside. Julia approached the door and knocked softly. She jumped back, startled, when Pete yanked the door open and rushed past her. He looked even more pale up close.

Julia moved to the window to watch Pete race into the barn. Hay started flying as he forked hay for the horses.

Julia moved into the room and over to Pete's dresser. She eased the top drawer open and saw five silver coins laying inside. She slid the drawer shut, called to her mother that she'd be out for a while, and went out to saddle her horse. Time to talk to Jake again.

———

Boone was well enough to be a pain in my neck again, but I supposed that was a good thing. Three days had passed since the gentleman bandit had taken a shot at him. The doc had kicked him out yesterday, told him to go home and rest. Boone didn't know how to do that, so he was sitting around the sheriff's office, wearing me out.

Alice Brenham came in, lucky for me. She interrupted him telling me for the fifth time how he had taken down the gentleman bandit. I had it memorized, but there was no stopping Boone. Alice took him off to the café for lunch and I heaved a sigh of relief.

Julia came in a few minutes later, and I knew that worried look. She pulled a chair close to the desk and told me right away what was on her mind.

"Pete's in trouble," she blurted. "I don't know exactly what, but he's scaring me. He left early this morning, then came back in maybe a half hour ago. He's pale as a ghost, his horse is all lathered up, and he won't talk to me."

She blew out a miserable breath and slumped back in

the chair. "He came in and put five dollars in a drawer when he came home. I don't know where he got that money. He gets a calf to raise sometimes, but when he sells it, the money goes in the bank. I don't know where he got five dollars in one morning."

I swung around and stood up, then sat on the corner of the desk, reaching to take her hand. Five dollars in one morning didn't sound like something Pete could make honestly. "No idea which direction he rode out or came back from?" I asked.

She shook her head. "He wasn't gone more than a few hours. He couldn't have gone too far."

I stood up and walked over to the window. "I'll look into it," I told her. "I'll check around, probably starting with the livery stable. If some horses have been ridden hard, my guess is that a couple of 'em will be at the stable."

I walked Julia outside, gave her a kiss, and promised I would be over for dinner. "Looking forward to it," I said. "Like always."

I kept the smile on my face and waved as she rode off, but the smile faded pretty fast. Truth was, it sounded like Pete had been in some kind of a holdup. I couldn't picture him doing it, but it was hard to explain otherwise.

I walked the few blocks to the livery stable. The kid Elmer was cleaning the stables. I ignored him and walked around the horses, stroking their necks, checking for the ones who were warm to the touch from recent riding. I found two.

The first was a little paint with floppy ears and a rough gait. I'd seen him often enough around town to know it belonged to Elmer. The second one, I couldn't be sure. It was a black gelding with no distinct markings on him. I checked the brand. It looked like a Circle R. There wasn't an outfit around here with that brand. Carr had ridden a black horse the other day, I remembered.

I looked up and saw that kid Elmer watching me. He was still shoveling, but he was checking on me from time to time, watching me move among the horses. Elmer had never given me any trouble, but that didn't mean there wouldn't be a first time. He'd shown up in town about six months ago, no family around here, and had worked at the stables the whole time.

I motioned for him to come over to me. He tossed the shovel aside and came slowly, looking back and forth from me to the sweating black gelding.

I pointed at the horse. "Who does he belong to?" I asked.

Elmer shrugged, avoiding my gaze. "I dunno," he mumbled.

I took a couple steps forward, getting uncomfortably close. Elmer backed up until he bumped up against the wall.

"Do you know how I do my job around here?" I asked.

Elmer stared at his boots. "I dunno," he said again.

"I stay on top of things," I answered. "I try to spot trouble before it gets up a head of steam. I look for things that don't look right to me. There's something here that doesn't look right to me."

I reached over and patted the black gelding on the neck. "Now," I continued, "you telling me you don't know who owns this horse, that doesn't seem right to me."

I moved in another half step. Elmer glanced left and right, fear in his eyes. He had nowhere to go.

"I could take you on back to the jail with me and make room in one of my cells until your memory improves. Come to think of it, while you're having a nice nap in the cell, I could go down to the telegraph office and send out your description. I could ask if you've ever been doing things you shouldn't have done."

"Carr. Johnny Carr. It's his horse," Elmer mumbled.

I backed off a couple of steps to give him a little room. "Good, your memory is better already," I told him. "What's this horse been doing this morning to get all sweaty like this?"

Elmer looked left and right, then went back to staring at his boots. "Exercise," he said. "Mr. Carr told me to take him out for a good run this morning. Yup." His Adam's apple bobbed up and down nervously.

"Uh-huh," I said. "And what about your horse? Why is your horse warm to the touch?"

"I ran him too. Exercise. He needed some exercise today."

"Mmmph," I said. I backed away, turning to look at him when I reached the gate to the stables. "I'm likely to come back and see you, Elmer," I told him. "I hope your memory keeps on getting better between now and then."

I walked back to the office, not liking the thoughts I was thinking. It was almost impossible to believe Pete Hawkins had been in some kind of stickup, but the trail led in that direction. I rounded the corner to see Boone, leaning on a cane, waiting for me outside the office.

"What?" I asked as I climbed the steps.

Boone jerked a thumb toward the office. "Rolf Bergen," he said. "Waitin' for you inside."

I wrinkled my brow, trying to place the name, which was familiar to me. "Help me out," I said.

"Sheriff over there to Kerrville, next county over," Boone reminded me.

Now it came to me. Bergen, white-haired gent, probably well up into his seventies. I suspected he was going to retire soon and just wanted to keep things peaceful until he did. Seemed like he had a good chance to me. Mostly farmers around there, most of 'em immigrants from Germany. Peaceful folks.

"What's he want?" I asked Boone.

He just shrugged. "You better talk to him yourself," was his only answer.

Rolf Bergen stood up when I walked in. "Trouble, Sheriff," he said. "We had a holdup at the bank in Kerrville. Had a man shot. Lots of money taken. I trailed 'em for a ways. They came through your town."

I sat down in my chair with a thump and let out a long, miserable sigh. It seemed like my worst dreams were coming true. I waved a hand at the empty chair next to the desk. "Tell me about it," I said.

CHAPTER 10

I grabbed a notebook and told Rolf to walk me through what had happened.

"CNB Bank, right on the edge of town," he said. "Four men came in, wearin' bandanas, according to the manager. They had a couple of gunny sacks, went around emptying drawers of money, then held a gun on the manager and made him open the safe. Had about a thousand dollars in there."

I raised my eyebrows a little. Cash money wasn't something farmers had a lot of, usually. "Do you think the bank really had that much?" I asked.

Bergen nodded. "Immigrant farmers," he answered. "They believe in savin' money and tucking it away. Anyway," he continued, "the manager, name of Bert Ferguson, pulled a pistol out of his desk drawer while the robbers were busy stuffing money in the sacks. Only had one clerk in the building, an' she was face down on the floor the whole time."

"They were on their way outta the building, then ran into old Kurt Samuels along the way. They knocked him down. He maybe got a bit of a look at them, but he was smart and stayed down. Bumped his head, but he's okay."

"This," he said, "is when it got a little messy. Bert Ferguson, the crazy manager, ran out and cut loose a couple shots at 'em whilst they were makin' their getaway. They, of course, turned around and shot back. Bert took one through the shoulder and got a nasty cut on his head when the shot slammed him up against the building."

"Bert has been sleepin' a lot since then, over at the doc's office. He comes out of it and talks a little now and then. Mostly makes sense, sometimes not. Doc said come back tomorrow, after he's had some rest.

"After I saw Bert," Rolf Bergen continued, "I tried tracking their horses. Bert said he thought there was two more of 'em holding horses. So, I found tracks for a bunch of horses. At least four or five. I trailed 'em all the way to Fredericksburg. One or two of 'em might have split off, but I'm sure most of 'em came to town over here."

He stopped and leaned back, folding his hands over his stomach.

"You want me to check around town, see if I can find out anything," I said. Actually, I had a good idea of where to look first, but I didn't like the idea of Rolf Bergen dumping the whole case on me.

He stared at me. "Well, yeah," he said. "They came to your county. I can't arrest 'em over here. You have to do this."

I rubbed the bridge of my nose and stared out the window. "Okay," I agreed. "I'll do some checking around here, and I want to talk to the bank manager and the old gent that got knocked down outside the bank."

"Kurt Samuels," he reminded me.

"Right," I said. "Kurt Samuels. But mostly, I want to talk to the bank manager. You said the doctor told you to come back tomorrow. I'll come over tomorrow morning. Can I meet you at the bank, then talk to Samuels and Ferguson after? I want to see how much they remember, and I'll have a couple questions for them."

Bergen nodded in satisfaction, got up, and went out. I watched him mount up and ride away. I knew that if this case got solved, I would have to be the one to do it.

I drummed my fingers on the desktop and stared out the window. Four robbers, plus two more holding the horses. The robbery had actually occurred in the next county over. I fished around in my desk drawer and pulled out the note telling me where I could get ahold of Leander McNelly by telegram. I folded it up and put it back in the drawer. I would go to Kerrville and look things over first.

That left me wondering whether I should tell Julia my suspicions about Pete's role in all of this. I decided to wait a little before I did that.

———

Johnny Carr moved out from his room at the boarding house, heading toward the livery stable. His head protested with every step he took. He remembered switching from beer to whiskey in the saloon last night. Or maybe it was when he left the first saloon and moved to the second one that he switched over.

He resented the hangover only a little. Yesterday's holdup had been worth celebrating. Twelve hundred dollars plus some change for the four of 'em. Everybody had agreed to keep two hundred for themselves and put the rest into the pot for Robber's Roost.

That had left two hundred in his pocket for spending however he liked—okay, it was a little less than that after last night, but at least he'd been smart enough not to buy a round for the house, or something stupid like that. Plus, it left almost four hundred for bringing booze into the Roost for that saloon he had promised everybody.

Four hundred was more than a good cowboy could make in a year. And they were only getting started. Turning the corner, Carr spotted the livery stable. He jammed his hat down a little more firmly and set his course for it.

Something was nagging him at the back of his brain, and he couldn't quite remember what it was. Just that it had seemed really important at the time. Carr stopped and put his hands on his hips, giving his headache a rest for a minute.

Carr stared down the road, trying to remember. It had seemed so important... Carr could see the livery stable kid with the big ears waving at him, but Carr turned his back. The kid could wait. He remembered the guy that he talked to at the saloon said he worked for the railroad. The Houston and Central Texas railroad. The guy had been so proud of it.

Now it came to him. Carr slapped his forehead at his own forgetfulness and immediately paid the price for that. The stabbing pain in his head caused him to bend over and grab his knees until it passed.

The guy had been working for the railroad, loading crates into a car. He and another guy had loaded ten heavy crates into a car bound for Austin, according to some papers the guy saw on one of the crates. Carr wasn't too sure this guy could read, but he swore up and down the papers had said Austin.

That was when things got interesting. They had dropped one crate, the guy said, and it split open. They were hustling to patch it up, seeing as how they didn't get paid for broken crates, when the guy saw something shiny inside and bent down on his knees to get a good look inside. Rifles! Brand-new Winchester '73 rifles, being shipped to Austin, probably for the new Texas Rangers, the guy figured. There were ten in the busted box.

Carr thought angrily about the old Henry rifle he carried around. Most folks couldn't get hold of the Winchester '73 yet, or couldn't pay for one if they did. McCabe had one—he'd noticed that right away. Probly only got it because he was a lawman.

What if he could get his hands on fifty of the Winchester '73s! He could recruit as many guys into his gang as he wanted! And they could hold off an Army from that stone house. Unless it really was the Army, and they brought a cannon. He didn't want to think about that.

Still, the guy had just loaded the guns the day before, and he was sure the train wasn't scheduled to leave for over a week. That gave Carr time to get the guys together, plus there was time to figure out how to stop that train. They would never expect a train robbery in the middle of nowhere.

Carr turned and started toward the livery stable again. The kid had quit waving, but he was standing at the entrance, looking up and down the road. Irritated, Carr picked up the pace a little to see what the kid was so excited about.

Elmer stepped out to meet him on the road, then put a hand on his shoulder to steer him out of sight, back in one of the stalls. Carr slapped the kid's hand away in irritation and stared at him.

"What?" was his only question.

"That sheriff, McCabe!" The words seemed to explode out of him. "He knows somethin' about that holdup, I think!"

Now he had Carr's attention, who forgot about the headache and focused on the kid.

"Why d'you think that?" he demanded. "Tell me what happened."

"He come up here yesterday, right after we got back from the stickup. He was walkin' around here, checking the horses to see which ones were still warm from bein' run. The only two was yours and mine. He asked why the horses was hot."

Elmer saw the thundercloud on Carr's face and took a step backward. "I told him I'd just been exercisin' them," he added defensively.

"Did he know the black gelding was my horse?" Carr asked, taking a step forward. "There's lots of black horses. That's one reason I got him." The look on Elmer's face gave him the answer.

"You told him!" He delivered a ringing slap to Elmer's face, who recoiled against the back wall of the stall.

"He woulda put me in jail!" Elmer howled. "He woulda figgered it out anyhow!"

Carr stepped back and forced himself to calm down. He still needed this kid's help for a while. "Okay, here's what you do," he said, keeping his voice as even as possible. "Keep your head down and stay out of trouble. Then, in another week or two, I've got a big job for you. Might take all night. Get somebody to cover the livery for you if you have to."

Elmer only nodded. He wasn't sure right now how he would do that, but he didn't need another slap. He waited to hear what else was coming.

"I need you to bring that kid, Pete, too." Elmer opened his mouth to protest but closed it when Carr drew back his hand for another slap.

"Tell him what you have to tell him. Remind him I'll come after his family and kill them if I have to. Get him here and ready to go when I tell you. Maybe he can be home by the time his family gets up the next day."

Elmer nodded dumbly and watched while Carr saddled the black gelding and led him out of the stables. He stared blankly at the wall after Carr rode away. For the first time, he admitted to himself how scared he was of this man.

———

The overnight rain had washed out the tracks Sheriff Bergen told me he'd followed from the robbery to the edge of Fredericksburg, but I didn't figure that mattered. He'd lost the trail when he reached the edge of town and there wasn't much chance I could pick it up a day later. Too many people had passed this way.

Bergen was waiting for me outside the bank, but he suggested we go over to the doctor's office to talk to the bank manager first. Apparently, he was awake and talking sense today. When we got there, Bergen made the introductions, reminding me the manager's name was Bert Ferguson. Ferguson grabbed my hand like he didn't plan on letting go.

"Didya catch those guys?" he half-yelled, his eyes bulging. "There was four of 'em you know. I got off a couple shots."

"That's what I heard," I said, eyeing his heavily bandaged shoulder, thinking how lucky this guy had been. "Tell me what happened."

Ferguson's account of the robbery didn't really help me. He said they came in, waving guns and taking money. From there, he just seemed to ramble, talking about opening the safe *because they had a gun up his nose* and changing the amount he said had been taken. First it was one thousand dollars, then two thousand. I was pretty sure he didn't really know.

He told me several times how he'd gotten an old Colt Navy revolver from his desk while they weren't looking and fired at them after they left the building.

"How about when they went to their horses?" I asked. "Were there men holding the horses?"

"Yeah, I think so," he said after a pause. "Dunno how many." His breathing was getting a little shallow. The doctor stepped in.

"He's had enough," the doctor told us.

We moved back outside. I figured that had been a total waste of time. I looked over at Bergen. "What else have you got for me?" I asked.

"We can go over to the bank. The clerk who was there will meet us, and old Kurt Samuels."

"Who?" The name didn't ring a bell for me.

"Old gent what got pushed over when they came outta the bank," he reminded me.

"Right." We rode back over to the bank, where the clerk was waiting for us. She cast nervous looks at the bank and asked not to go inside with us.

"I'll just answer your questions out here, if that's okay," she said. "I haven't been back in there yet."

The clerk wasn't as wild-eyed as her manager, but she didn't give me much to work with, either. She said they came in, walked over to her cage, and pointed a gun at her. They told her to put all the money in her tray into a burlap sack, so she did. They told her to lie down on the floor and not move, so that's what she did.

They told the manager to open the safe. She heard some arguing. She hadn't looked up. It sounded to her like the safe was opened eventually, then it got quiet for a while. Then there were gunshots. Someone fired one shot inside, she was sure of that. It sounded to her like the rest were coming from outside. She stuck her nose out the door too soon and got shot at. By the time she finally got back up and went outside, old Kurt Samuels was on his feet, looking after Bert Ferguson, her manager, who was down and bleeding. She had jumped on her horse and ridden to get the doctor.

The clerk left. She hadn't told me anything I didn't know before, except somebody had fired one shot inside. I wasn't sure it mattered who had fired that one. We went inside and scouted around. The safe was closed back up, of course. The rest of the place hadn't been straightened up since the robbery, but we didn't find anything except papers scattered on the floor.

I found one bullet hole in the wall, so I dug the bullet out and put it in my pocket. I wasn't sure if that would help me or not.

We moved back outside, and Bergen pointed at an elderly, white-haired man shuffling down the road toward us.

"That's Kurt Samuels," he said. "Walks everywhere he goes."

I waited until Samuels reached us, and Bergen made the introductions again.

"Tell me what happened," I said, wondering if today had been a total waste.

Samuels stroked his beard. "Well," he drawled. "First thing I noticed was a couple kids holding a bunch of hosses over there." He pointed to the dusty ground next to the bank.

That got my attention. "You said kids," I pointed out. "How young were they?"

Samuels scratched his head and thought that one over. "I dunno, mebbe twenty," he said. "I could see their faces a little, and they was skinny, like most kids. Just sittin' over there, holdin' several hosses. I guess four hosses, on account that's how many varmints come outta the bank."

"Could you see their hair?" I asked, leaning forward. "Did one of them have red hair?"

Samuels squinted his eyes and pondered. "Can't say," he concluded. "They was both wearin' hats. Black hats."

"Okay," I said. "Go on. You said there were four of them coming out of the bank."

"Yup," he agreed. "Four of 'em busted outta the bank an' they shoved me down on the way out. Wearin' hats and bandanas over their faces. Then ol' crazy Bert come out, whangin' away at 'em with that old pistol of his. They fired back and knocked Bert down. Mounted up an' rode off." His face screwed up in disgust.

"Yankees!" he said. He leaned over and spat in the dust, grumbling under his breath.

"Yankees?" The question popped out of my mouth

while old Kurt was still spitting. "Why did you say they were Yankees?"

"Belt buckles." He leaned over and spat again, just as disgusted as before. "Had them Army belt buckles, two of 'em did. Noticed it when they shoved me down. Sittin' on my fanny, saw them belt buckles right in front of my face. US Army buckles. Bluebelly belt buckles."

I looked over at Sheriff Bergen, who just shrugged. "First I've heard that," he said. "We don't have hardly any Union veterans around these parts."

"Good thang, too," Kurt growled, leaning over to spit again.

I looked around, trying to think of anything else to ask him, but I couldn't think of any more questions. I thanked the old man, and he went back down the road, mumbling about bluebellies until he was out of earshot. I didn't tell him I had fought for the North myself.

I thanked Bergen and told him I would let him know what I could find out. I mounted up and turned Sherman down the road back to Fredericksburg. There was a lot to think about, and none of it was good. Two kids had held the horses. There was a good chance one of those kids was Pete.

Then there was old Kurt's statement that two of them wore US Army belt buckles. Johnny Carr hadn't been wearing one, I was pretty sure of that, but maybe he had some buddies from the Army down here to rob banks and whatever else?

It wasn't a crazy idea. Quantrill and some of those boys up in Kansas were Confederate vets who went a little crazy after the war. Same thing could happen to Union soldiers. Most of the South had little left to rob after the war, but Texas was different. It was the cattle money that had helped folks down here.

By the time I reached Fredericksburg, I figgered I was in need of some help. This was bigger than me and my county, if I was right. I fished in my pocket and found the slip of paper I was looking for. I detoured to the telegraph office. Time to get in touch with McNelly.

CHAPTER 11

WAGON'S PLAN

Wagon had grudgingly accepted the whiskey a guy named Dennison had offered him—the same guy who had almost blown his head off just a few minutes ago. It had taken a lot of cutting back and forth in the scorching sun, searching for this Robber's Roost hideout. How was he supposed to know he was expected to come in waving a white flag?

Dennison had held a gun on him even after they got to this huge stone house. He kept on holding the gun until Wagon produced the note from Carr. That's when Dennison had given him the whiskey, turned his back and walked off to read the note.

Finally, Dennison turned around, looking pretty sour, from where Wagon was standing. Dennison tossed him a burlap sack and pointed to the room next door. "Go in the pantry over there and get yourself some vittles. There's bread, jerky, some beans. Fill up your canteen. You'll be riding out as soon as I get the others."

Wagon opened his mouth to protest. He had first

taken the train for four days, then ridden another hard day to get here. He'd been planning on sleeping for the rest of the day, plus tonight. How was he supposed to just mount up and head out? Even his horse needed some rest.

"You can swap out your horse out in the corral. The other boys will show you which one you can have," Dennison said. His eyes never left Wagon's face.

Wagon shut his mouth, cutting off the complaining he'd been planning on. He didn't need the muzzle of that Colt staring him down anymore.

The two other guys came out, introduced themselves as Harris and Wood, then took Wagon out to the corral to swap horses. Wagon noticed they didn't cotton to Dennison any more than he did. That made him feel a little better. Maybe they would be interested in what he'd been planning on the way up.

Wagon was thinking he was a part of the gang now. He'd met the big boss down in Texas, who had trusted him to come to the hideout up here and bring a couple more of the boys. This was all about making some money, and during his years in Texas, Wagon had noticed a couple of small-town banks that looked ripe for the picking. He'd just never had anybody to help him out and back him up.

Harris and Wood showed him a buckskin that looked at least as good as the horse he was leaving behind, so Wagon decided not to complain about switching mounts. Harris started to brag about robbing settlers coming down the Santa Fe Trail. Wagon patted his shirt pocket, where he'd written down some information about a little place called Hico, Texas. Maybe he would see eye-to-eye with these boys.

He had ridden through the town of Hico, not too long ago. It was bigger than he'd thought, with a general store, a cotton mill, and several other businesses. It had a post office, but only one saloon. Apparently, the Methodist Church was pretty big in town. And no bank.

That one had gotten his attention. He hung around town for a while, and it looked to him like folks went to the general store to get money. The owner would disappear into the back for a while, then come out with cash money when folks asked. Wagon figured there was some kind of strong room back there. Easy, in other words.

Wagon mounted up with Harris and Wood, and they took off for the train stop at the end of the line in Kansas. After switching to the KATY line, Wagon would get off in Dallas, then he would take them right through Hico. It was out of their way, but it ought to be worth their while. They would get to Waco in plenty of time to meet Carr. No reason they couldn't stop off and make a little money on the way. Carr didn't even need to know.

Dennison watched them go, his resentment boiling over once they got out of sight. Whatever big plans Carr had going on down in Texas, they had left him out of it. Dennison wasn't sure what that meant. Did it mean Carr didn't trust him? Maybe Carr planned to get rid of him.

Either way, he didn't have to sit here and watch over an empty hideout the whole time. There were plenty of stragglers up there on the trail, just waiting to get picked clean. The Army should have settled down since the last raid. Dennison would find himself a straggler on the trail with some good horses and a heavy-looking wagon. He wouldn't have to share this with anybody.

Pete had saved his least favorite job for the last. Cleaning out the horse stalls in the barn was a job he handed off to his little brother Isaac whenever he could talk the kid into it, but today wasn't one of those days. One look overhead told him it was getting late in the afternoon— maybe four o'clock. He couldn't put it off any longer.

First, he turned the three horses in the barn out to the corral, then trudged back into the barn, picking up a rake along the way. After just a minute or two of raking out the stalls, a quiet hiss from the hayloft behind him caused Pete to jump.

"Pssst! Pete!"

Pete dropped the rake and whirled. He was both shocked and relieved to see the familiar red hair and freckled face of Elmer. He stared in astonishment. It had been more than a week since the robbery. Pete had made a point of avoiding Elmer since then.

"How'd you get in here? What are you doing up there?"

Elmer dropped down from the hayloft, glancing nervously over his shoulder at the open barn door. He moved toward the back of the barn, motioning for Pete to follow. He positioned himself behind a stack of hay bales.

"There's another job for us, holding horses," Elmer said in hushed tones. "Tomorrow night—I know that's your free night. This one will take a while, but you can be back before anybody else is up. Pays three dollars this time."

Elmer wasn't really sure what Carr would pay, but he knew his job was to get Pete out there with him. For that matter, he wasn't all that confident they would be home by sunup, but he was prepared to promise whatever it took. His gut told him it would be dangerous to disappoint Carr.

Pete's mouth thinned down, and his jaw set in a stubborn line. "I'm not doing any more jobs for Carr," he growled. "Last time turned out to be a lot more than holding horses. I've been looking over my shoulder, waiting for Jake to show up anytime, haulin' me off to jail."

"This one will be different," Elmer wheedled. "No more bank jobs, Carr told me." The last sentence was a lie, but if this turned out to be another bank robbery, it would be too late for Pete to back out by the time he figured out what was going on.

Pete took a step back, shaking his head from side to side. "Nope, I'm out", he said firmly. "You work for Carr. I'm not going to anymore."

"Carr won't let you stop. He'll come after your family. He told me to tell you that." The words came out of Elmer with a rush, and for the first time, he had the convincing sound of a man telling the truth.

Pete's head dropped, and his shoulders sagged. Carr had said the same thing to him when they parted ways after the Kerrville holdup. He'd spent the time since convincing himself that wouldn't happen. Now, a little voice inside him said that Elmer was right. Carr would come after everybody he loved if he didn't go along.

He looked up at Elmer, his eyes burning with anger and resentment. "Why'd you get me into this?" he demanded. When he got only a shrug as an answer, he knew that Elmer was probably also in a lot deeper than he cared to be.

Pete heaved a sigh of resignation. "This is the last one I'll do," he insisted.

Elmer shrugged again. "Sure," he said. He was way past knowing what he could and couldn't promise. He had a pretty good idea it would be deadly to say no to Carr.

"Okay," Pete mumbled. "Where do I need to be and when?"

"Meet me at the livery stable tomorrow," came the quick answer. "Around this time of day. Carr will meet us." Elmer ducked out the side door of the barn as soon as he finished talking. Pete could hear the hoofbeats moving away.

Pete slid down to his heels, bracing himself up against the side of the barn. He stared at his boots, trying to decide what he could do about this. Tomorrow, he would come with Elmer. He had to. This time, though, he planned to bring a gun. He knew where there was an old revolver, tucked away in a drawer in the chest over in the corner. He stood, walked over to the chest, and pulled out the gun. He stuffed it down into one boot and went back to cleaning the stalls.

———

Julia paused and leaned on the hoe, wondering, as always, how her garden grew so many weeds so fast. She wiped a sleeve across her forehead and tried to estimate how long the rest of this would take her. She had promised to cook dinner tonight and she was running out of time.

Movement behind the barn caught her eye and she took a couple of steps to her left to see who was riding away. She looked just in time to see the rider clap a battered old hat down over an unruly pile of red hair. There was only one head of hair that red anywhere around here. It had to be Elmer. What, she wondered, was he doing out here?

Julia set the hoe down and walked slowly to the open door of the barn. She peeked around the corner and saw Pete, his back turned to her, cleaning out the horse stalls. She pulled back out of sight and returned to her garden.

A secret meeting between Elmer and Pete couldn't possibly be good, she was sure of that. The question was, could she do anything about it?

After hoeing two more rows, she came to a decision. Tomorrow night was Pete's night off, when he usually rode to town in Fredericksburg. She would have to follow him. In her heart of hearts, she was sure that Pete was in serious trouble.

––––––––

Miles Jamison had heard enough grumbling from Blondie and Beard to last him for a while. He called a break to the hard labor and slumped down over a fallen tree, reaching for his canteen and wiping the sweat dripping down his face.

He couldn't really blame them for grumbling. When they got louder about it than usual, he barked at them to shut up, but that was just to keep them in line. He couldn't answer the questions about why Johnny Carr wasn't here, helping them. Jamison suspected Carr just didn't want to get his hands dirty. Or, get hisself this sweaty in the Texas heat.

This had all started when Carr had shown up at Jamison's favorite waterin' hole, there in Austin. He knew Carr must have ridden hard and fast to get there. He was all lathered up about Jamison taking his crew and findin' a place to hold up a train. Had to happen by nine a.m. the day after next, he kept saying.

Jamison had poured him a couple of beers and asked a few questions until Carr calmed down a bit. "What train? Where? What's gonna be on the train?"

The answers had been pretty slow in coming, it reminded Jamison of goin' to the dentist last time. Three teeth yanked out, one at a time. Jamison winced at the memory.

"Houston and Central Texas railroad," Carr had finally answered. "Due to arrive in Austin by ten o'clock the day after tomorrow. You've got to take your crew at least an hour south of Austin, where nobody'll bother us," Carr had said, "and build somethin' on those tracks to derail that train, so we can rob it."

Jamison had pressed him about what was on the train that was so all-fired important to rob. "Gold?" he'd asked.

That's when Carr had gotten real cagey. "Mebbe some gold," he'd said. "Something that will help the gang make a lot more money. You'll see. Plus, you can rob the passengers for whatever they've got."

And so, Jamison had rousted out Blondie and Beard before sunup this morning, and they had ridden south for about an hour, following along the train tracks, looking for a good spot, only Jamison hadn't told them what was going on until he had found a place that suited him.

He needed a place where the train had to slow down,

maybe from pulling up a long, slow rise. Also, and most important, he needed a place where the train had to round a curve, someplace where the engineer couldn't see around the bend until it was too late.

They had ridden at least an hour, scouting places, before Jamison had called a halt. He'd found his place, just like he'd pictured it in his head. The train had to pull up a long, slow rise for several hundred yards, then take a pretty sharp bend around a curve. A big stand of oak trees blocked the view.

That's where Jamison had called a halt and had given Blondie and Beard the good news and the bad news. The good news: they were going to rob a train. The bad news: he couldn't tell them what was on the train, and they were going to have to drag logs and boulders across the track before the next train came. That's when he'd lifted the tarp on his packhorse and tossed several sharp axes down on the ground.

Now, several hours later, they were making headway. They'd been lucky enough to find a few dead logs, hitched them to the horses, and pulled them across the tracks. He was taking Carr's word for it there weren't any more trains coming until morning. Chopping down a couple more trees had been back-breaking work.

Jamison looked at the calluses forming on his hands. The second tree had nearly taken him down. He hadn't expected it to fall in his direction and he'd barely gotten out of the way. They had to hitch up the horses and tie ropes to those two trees they had chopped down. Jamison had decided to call it a day after they hauled those trees across the tracks. Blondie and Beard had done about all they were likely to do today.

In the morning, Jamison figured there were a few

small boulders they could push across the tracks to anchor down the logs. That should be enough to stop or derail the train. Then they should have enough guns on hand to steal whatever Carr wanted to steal. Whatever it was, it better be worth all this trouble.

Jamison stood and moved to get his horse. He wasn't expecting Carr until morning. If he didn't show, they would just take whatever they felt like from that train.

————

Wagon led the way into Hico, walking his horse slowly down Main Street, and stopped at a café across the street from the general store. Harris and Wood followed behind, but they took their time. Harris tethered his horse at the post office, and Wood stopped at the general store. They met inside the café. The plan was to not attract any attention while they watched the general store and made plans.

There was a board leaning against the wall near the entrance of the café with a sheet of paper nailed to it. Harris walked to the board, looked it over, and came back to the table.

"Looks like they've got steak, chili, bread, and beans," he announced. "Apple pie and coffee." When a kid emerged from the back and approached the table, they ordered all of it. The kid mumbled something and turned to leave. Harris reached over and grabbed his arm to stop him.

"I need to ask the sheriff about somethin'," Harris said, feeling pleased with himself for being so sneaky. "Where can I find him?"

The kid looked completely confused. "Sheriff?" he

asked, scratching his head. "We don't got a sheriff around here. Not in Hico, anyways."

Wood's face broke out in a smile, and Harris kicked him under the table. He turned back to look at the kid. "Well," he said, "this here is an important question. Where do I have to go to talk to the sheriff?"

"Hamilton," the kid said, pointing south. "Mebbe a day's ride, south of here." He turned and shuffled into the kitchen.

They watched the general store for almost an hour, stuffing themselves on the food. While they watched, a woman walked into the store and came out about ten minutes later. The kid from the café walked over and came back, lugging a bag of flour into the kitchen. Wagon and the two others moved down to the saloon after they'd eaten, where they worked up a little courage with some whiskey.

When they emerged from the saloon, they saw a buggy tied up in front of the general store. They stopped and watched. A farmer came out and threw a few bags into the buggy. He walked back into the store and came back out a few minutes later, stuffing something into his pockets.

"Money," Wagon mumbled. "Just like I told ya."

Harris and Wood nodded. They waited while the farmer pulled the buggy around and left town.

Leaving their horses where they were, the three of them crossed the street. Pausing outside the door, they drew their guns and filed through the door. A woman was pushing a drawer shut behind the counter. Her mouth dropped open in surprise when she saw them.

A door behind the woman opened, and a man came out. He stopped when he saw the guns.

"This here is a stickup," Harris announced. "Go back there and open your safe."

The woman gathered her breath to scream, but Wagon jumped forward and aimed his pistol at her head. "I wouldn't do that, ma'am," he said. He moved around the counter and wrapped his arm around her neck, gun to her head. "Go open the safe," he told the man. "Don't waste no time doin' it."

CHAPTER 12

TRAILING PETE

Wagon waited where he was while Harris and Wood advanced on the shopkeeper.

"What's yer name?" Harris asked.

The shopkeeper's eyes never left his wife. Wagon still held his gun to her head. "Edwards," he answered. "Hal Edwards."

Harris thumbed back the hammer on his Colt. "Well, Hal Edwards," he said, giving him a push toward the back door, "we know you've got a safe back there with some money in it. Let's you and me go and do somethin' about that."

Edwards led the way to the back room and knelt in front of a small iron safe. His hands were steady as he dialed a few numbers, pulled the door open, and stood back.

Wood, holding a bag he'd grabbed in the store, knelt and cackled when he saw a pile of bills and some gold coins. He shoveled everything he saw into the bag, stood, and nodded at Harris, a huge grin splitting his face.

Harris grabbed the bag and pointed at the door. "You

go out first," he told Edwards. "We don't want no surprises when we come out the door."

Edwards moved out of the room and to the countertop. He laid both hands on top of it. Harris nodded at Wagon. "Bring her to the front door with us," he commanded.

Wagon walked toward the front door with the woman, followed by Wood. Harris, still clutching the bag, backed away from the counter and moved to the door. "We're gonna let go of her out by the front door and get outta here," he told Edwards. "Don't try nothin'."

Edwards nodded, watching as they pushed his wife to the front door, then turned and ran for their horses. "Get back inside, Mary," he said quietly. She backed into the store slowly while Edwards bent and pulled a shotgun out from under the counter. "Stay in here," he said, then ducked and held low as he trotted to the front door.

———

Out in the street, Harris, still holding the money, ran to his horse, untied it, and swung aboard. He turned his horse to the south. They were headed south out of town. Nothing had changed there. He looked over his shoulder. Wagon, showing surprising moves for a man his size, untied his horse, turned, and leaped into the saddle. He moved out to join Harris.

Wood, whose horse was just north of the general store, trotted to his mount, still grinning from ear to ear. He grabbed to untie the reins from the hitching rail, missing the first time. He stopped to get them untied, then pulled his horse around and climbed aboard.

Wood kicked his horse in the ribs and trotted past the

general store. Too late, he saw Edwards coming out of the door with a shotgun. He swore as he clawed to get his gun out of the holster. The shotgun boomed and he felt a huge punch in his stomach. Tumbling backward out of the saddle, he stared up at the blue sky until it slowly faded away.

Harris swung his horse around in time to see Wood hit by the shotgun blast. He reached for his gun, but Edwards cut loose with the other barrel before Harris cleared the leather. Harris felt a sharp sting in his arm. Down the street, he saw a man spill out of the post office, raising a rifle in their direction.

Harris and Wagon laid out low over their horses' ears and spurred them forward. One rifle shot, then another whistled over their heads as they galloped out of town.

————

Edwards trotted out from the general store and stood over the dead man in the middle of the street. Two men carrying rifles ran to meet him there. The kid from the café burst out the front door. "Dad?" he shouted frantically. "Mom?"

Hal Edwards threw an arm around his son. "We're okay," he said. "Nobody got hurt except this varmint, here." He nudged Wood with his boot. "This 'un ain't going anywhere." He raised his arm to stop two men who were mounting up.

"I don't want nobody gettin' themselves killed chasin' those two," he said. "Ain't worth it." He looked over at his son. "Timmy," he said, "it's a day's ride down to the sheriff in Hamilton, but it's only two days ride to Waco. I trust Fred Waters more, the sheriff down in Waco. Plus, he can get more help if'n he needs it. Fork your horse over there and ride to Waco. Tell 'em what happened."

Timmy led his horse around to the street and took the bag of food his mother shoved at him. Hal Edwards walked over and laid a hand on his shoulder. "Can you describe those guys?" he asked. "I saw 'em go into the café earlier."

Getting a nod in reply, Edwards sent the boy on his way. "Go slow at first," he said. "Just in case you're headed the same way. Let 'em get ahead of you." Then he walked over and stared down at Wood. "Now," he said, to nobody in particular, "I've got to bury this coyote." He sighed and walked into his store to get a shovel.

————

Pete was suspicious of her, that much Julia felt sure of, since that incident when he caught sight of her watching him at the livery stable in town. That left her with some tough choices today. Pete had taken his horse out to work on the southern fences this morning, but she had noticed that his saddlebag looked pretty full. On a hunch, she checked the drawer in the barn with the spare pistol—it was gone.

It occurred to her that trailing Pete from in front might be the best way to do this for a while. If he was headed for trouble, she reasoned, he was probably going to see Elmer at the livery stable first. If she reached town before Pete did and found a way to watch the livery stable without being seen, that might be the way to keep track of Pete without him knowing it, and maybe keep him out of deep water.

Her mind made up, Julia made up a small pack with a

bit of food, a blanket, and a slicker in case it rained. She moved some things aside in the bottom of a drawer and pulled out a Colt Navy revolver. She had bought it just a couple years ago, when she had been forced to defend herself and her family. She had practiced with it and knew she could use it if she had to. Julia put the Navy Colt into the pack, carried it out to the barn, and tied it on her horse.

Retracing her steps, Julia paused when she saw the Henry rifle, leaned against a corner. She decided against taking it. She hoped to get Pete away from Elmer and whatever it was they had planned without gunfire. If that didn't work out, maybe the Colt was enough.

Moving to the kitchen, Julia took a seat and watched as her mother Jeanne started mopping the floor.

"I'm going to go into town," she announced.

"Okay." Jeanne barely paused as she mopped. She assumed Julia was going in to see Jake McCabe, which was fine with her.

"I might get a room at the boarding house in town and stay over," Julia said impulsively. She hadn't thought about that before, but she didn't want anybody worrying if she didn't come home until morning.

Jeanne paused this time, surprise showing on her face. Julia staying over in town would be a first. Still, she knew of no one more level-headed than her daughter. She pushed a wisp of hair away from her forehead. "All right," she said. "Jake's in town, isn't he?" she asked as an afterthought. "He's not on a trip, is he?"

"He's in town," Julia confirmed.

Reassured, Jeanne went back to mopping. "See you when you get back, then, sweetie."

Julia took a route to town that bypassed the southern pastures of the ranch. The last thing she wanted was to run into Pete before she even got started. Reaching town about fifteen minutes later, she looped around the livery stable, tethered her horse in the trees well back of the road, and concealed herself behind a large pecan tree. She settled down to watch the livery stable.

Elmer's red hair was easily visible as he moved back and forth in the stable, but he seemed to be alone in there. Julia moved over to her saddlebag, pulled out a chunk of cheese and settled back behind the pecan tree, determined to make an afternoon of it if she needed to.

Five minutes later, everything had changed. First, the same man came in she had seen talking to Elmer and Pete the last time she'd been here. Johnny Carr, Jake had told her. Maybe an innocent man looking for cows to drive north, but maybe not. Julia had her doubts. Minutes later, Pete rode in. Julia stashed her food back in the saddlebag and watched intently.

Within another few minutes, the three of them had mounted up and ridden out. A kid Julia didn't recognize emerged from the back of the stable, and appeared to be covering Elmer's job for him. Julia mounted up, pulled up her hair, and stuffed it under a man's hat she had brought with her. She settled in to follow from a discreet distance as the three men ahead struck the trail out of town, moving west.

They were moving at a brisk pace up there, cantering due west. Julia recognized the trail as the one that led directly to Austin. Worried about being seen, she hung back whenever the trial climbed up a slight rise. After an hour on the trail, she began to worry less about being seen. They never seemed to check their backtrail, seemingly just intent on getting where they were going.

The heat of the afternoon came and went, and Julia stayed on their trail. When they stopped to water their horses in a creek that crossed the trail, she hung back, pulling into the trees. She stopped to give her horse a short drink when they moved out, fearful she would lose them.

As the sun began to set, she tried to assess how long she had been following them. At least six hours, by her best guess, and they were still moving at a brisk pace. She tried to remember how much moonlight she would have tonight. The moon had been at least half full the last couple of nights, so she would have some light to work with. How long, she wondered, did they intend to keep going without pulling over for some rest and sleep?

The moon began to climb overhead, and Julia reached into her saddlebag for a roll and the rest of the cheese she had started eating back in Fredericksburg. That seemed like several days ago. She took a few swigs of water, stopped to water her horse, then grimly returned to the trail.

Just when she felt sure they would ride into Austin, Carr, Pete, and Elmer jogged to the southeast on a very faint trail. This, she knew, would take them south of Austin. She couldn't imagine where they were going. At the risk of being seen, she urged her horse forward to close a bit of the gap. They were much harder to follow by moonlight on this narrow, winding trail.

By the time another two hours or more had passed, she felt herself beginning to doze in the saddle. They had at least slowed to a walk by this time. Julia pinched her arm several times in an effort to stay awake.

She was startled when the trail gave way to a wide, treeless path, leaving the trail and pointing almost due north and south. When she finished rounding a bend in the trail and moved forward, she was doubly startled to see they had come to a railroad track.

Urging her horse forward a little farther, she swung her gaze both north and south. There, in the moonlight, she could make out the three of them, moving south along the side of the tracks. Julia swung down, feeling stiff and achy from more than ten hours in the saddle. She took another look to the south. There was no way she could continue to track them tonight. She would be far too obvious following the railroad track with no trees or curves in the trail to shield her from their sight.

With no other choices left to her, Julia pulled her horse back into the trees at the side of the tracks, hobbled her horse, and spread her blanket out on the ground. She would have to resume tracking at first light, but she would have to be very careful. If they had pulled off into the trees on either side of the tracks and she rode past, she had a pretty good idea how much danger she would be in.

————

Carr estimated they had ridden south from the railroad tracks for about forty-five minutes. According to what they had discussed, they must be close to the spot where Jamison was preparing to stop the train. Carr held up his hand to stop his little party, moved his horse into the trees, and swung down.

They would camp here until morning, he decided. Not that morning was far off, but he wasn't fool enough to ride into another man's camp in the dark. He'd known several soldiers who had died that way during the war. Word was that Stonewall Jackson had died that way. He didn't plan to follow suit.

Elmer and Pete rode in behind him and spread out their blankets after seeing to their own horses as well as Carr's horse. Feeling bold, Elmer looked over at Carr as he settled down into the blankets.

"Are we gonna rob a train?" Elmer asked.

Carr propped up on one elbow and said nothing, but gave Elmer a long, hard stare. Elmer laid down on his blanket and said nothing else.

Pete laid down and stared up at the sky. He knew he wouldn't be able to sleep tonight. It was a train robbery, he was sure. This time, he told himself, he had to do something about it, even if it got him killed. He was no outlaw, and it was time to prove it.

Pete came awake, startled, a couple of hours later. A boot toe shoved into his ribs had done the trick. He didn't have to look—he knew it was Carr that had kicked him in the ribs. He stood without a word and packed up his blanket. He could smell bacon frying and moved over to the campfire, surprised he had been allowed to sleep this long.

Johnny Carr led the way south right after they'd had bacon and biscuits and washed it down with a little coffee. Half an hour later, Carr heard voices, mostly swearing, along with some thumping noises. He held up a hand to slow the pace, then proceeded cautiously forward. Five minutes later, he pulled up, surveying with satisfaction the work Jamison and his boys had done to stop this morning's train.

Beyond a curve in the tracks to the south and at the top of a small rise, several logs had been dragged across the tracks. As he watched, Jamison and the two others were rolling small boulders over to the tracks, no doubt planning to roll them onto the tracks behind the logs. Jamison looked up, saw them, and walked over, his face pouring sweat despite the early hour.

Jamison stopped beside Carr's horse, waiting for him to say something. Carr nodded in satisfaction, pulled his watch from his vest pocket, and checked the time. It was seven-thirty. He returned the watch to his pocket and stared down at Jamison.

"Looks good," he said curtly. "I figger you've got about an hour to finish getting ready for the train."

Jamison barely blinked, returning Carr's stare. Finally, he glanced behind Carr at the two boys waiting on their horses. "Do ya think you boys can help?" he rasped.

Carr waved an arm at Elmer and Pete. "Get over there and help 'em with those rocks," he barked. Catching the resentful look on Jamison's face, he dismounted, walked over, and gave a little push here and there as the others strained with the rocks.

At eight thirty exactly, Carr called a halt to the work, and they all retreated into the trees, pacing nervously and waiting for the train to arrive. Pete, while the others were all concentrated on the train, moved to his saddlebags, eased out his pistol, and tucked it into his waistband, under his vest.

The nervous silence was broken twenty minutes later when a train whistle sounded down beyond the curve in the tracks. Carr and his party ducked down and watched from under the trees.

The train rounded the bend under a full head of steam, but that changed immediately when the engineer saw the logs and boulders in his path. A shrill whistle sounded, then came the awful grinding shriek of brakes being applied. The sudden braking caused a coupling to snap about halfway down the length of the train, where the momentum of the cars combined with the bend in the tracks caused about twenty cars to leap the tracks and plunge down the hill and into the trees.

Back at the front of the train, the engineer kept the pressure on the brakes, but he knew he didn't have room to stop. He threw his arm over his eyes as sparks flew and the engine struck the barrier with a tremendous crash. The deafening noise echoed down the length of the train as each car slammed into the car in front of it. The decoupled cars kept rolling down the hill until they smashed into the trees.

At last, both halves of the train came to rest. Steam poured out of the engine, and they began to hear moans and cries from inside the cars. Pieces of metal landed on the ground by the tracks, some of them coming close to the outlaws hiding in the trees.

To a man, all the robbers in the trees stared, dumbfounded, at the destruction they had caused. Carr finally stood and waved the men forward. "Check the freight cars first," he barked. "We're looking for cash, maybe gold, maybe paper. And," he said, pausing for effect, "we're looking for Winchester '73 rifles."

CHAPTER 13

McNelly

Pete stood, his mouth open, frozen with the shock of what he had just witnessed. After arriving, under Carr's watchful eye, he had helped roll a couple of boulders onto the tracks, but his mind had been at work, trying to think of anything he could do to stop the train crash. When the destruction came, it stunned him.

He had made sure he was on the far-left flank of the outlaws, he was the one closest to the barricade they had put up across the tracks. When the engine had rounded the curve, he had ripped off his bandana and waved it. With other outlaws fixated on the train, only the engineer had seen him. And Pete was sure the man had seen him. He just didn't have enough time to react.

Now, with the crash still echoing in his ears, he heard Carr giving orders to board the train and rob passengers and baggage. His brain told him to get out of there. Pete turned, sprinted to his horse, and jumped on. He reined the horse around and leaned over, pounding the animal with his heels and urging him to get both of them out of there.

Things began to happen too fast for his mind to process. The back half of the train, off to his right, was just coming to rest. With a little luck, he could make his escape before anybody looked around.

"Hey!"

It was a shout from one of the robbers. Pete glanced back and saw the one they called Blondie yelling at him, then reaching to pull his rifle from the scabbard.

Pete kicked his horse in the ribs again. He was already leaning as far over as he could. He yanked his pistol from his waistband and fired a wild shot over his shoulder. Then he saw his sister, Julia. How was that possible? Now he heard voices from two different directions. Blondie was still yelling at him to stop. Julia, in front of him, was yelling at him to get out of there.

He heard two gunshots almost at once. Julia had pulled out a pistol and fired as he went by. The bullet whistled past him. He felt a thump in his shoulder before he heard the second gunshot, coming from behind. As he tumbled out of the saddle, he knew Blondie had shot him.

———

The night had passed slowly for Julia, even considering she had been rolled up in her blanket for only a few hours. Any noise in the woods brought her halfway to a sitting position, and she did not know how to free Pete from the mess he was in. She could only trail them and watch for her chance.

A mockingbird's shrill morning song brought her out

of the light doze she was in. A quick glance around told her it was only a few minutes past sunup. She had time for a biscuit and a little beef jerky before she saddled up and moved out.

She needed to stay in the trees at the side of the tracks but felt better moving in the gray dawn light. They had a big head start on her this morning, but she could see some hoofprints over near the tracks, giving her a little confidence she hadn't lost their trail.

Julia estimated she had been on the trail for about an hour before she thought she heard voices. She pulled up and listened for a few minutes, but now she heard nothing. She shrugged and urged her horse forward again.

She wondered where Carr and his men were going. Following the trail to Austin made sense. Following train tracks south made none.

Now she heard another sound, and it was unmistakable—there was a train coming. Julia pulled her horse farther over into the woods and kept moving forward. She came to a break in the trees and realized she was looking at a bend in the tracks.

As the train rounded the bend, she was focused on the train. Gradually, she took in the bigger picture in front of her, and her eyes widened at the realization of what was about to happen.

A barricade of logs and rocks formed a solid barrier on the tracks directly in front of her. To her left, only forty or fifty yards away, Pete was standing and waving his red bandana. Her gaze swung right, and she saw several other men, crouched down and waiting for the crash.

The train whistle sounded, then sparks flew from the wheels and the train uncoupled in the middle. The engine rolled forward, brakes screeching, then collided with the barrier. She covered her ears at the sound of the crash. Men to her right scattered to escape the back half of the train, now off the tracks.

Off to her right, Pete was moving. He jumped on his horse and kicked the animal into a run, heading straight for her. She heard a shout and looked to see one of the outlaws pulling a rifle free of the scabbard and lifting it at Pete.

Julia was already reaching into her saddlebag for the Navy Colt. She wished she had brought the Henry rifle. No time for that now. She lifted the Navy Colt, holding it with both hands to steady it down, then squeezed the trigger. She felt the shock in her arms and heard the roar of two guns, almost at the same time.

The man in front of her stumbled backward, his hat coming off and his hair flying as he hit the ground. He was down, his rifle spilling to the ground beside him. Now there was another noise, this time behind her.

She wheeled around to see Pete on the ground, holding his shoulder and trying to rise. There was blood coming from his shoulder, and his horse had trotted off into the woods. Julia kneed her horse forward and jumped down, giving Pete support as he tried to stand.

"Get on my horse," she told him.

Pete moaned but struggled to his knees. His mouth moved, but no words came. Now he looked over her shoulder and his eyes widened. Julia felt a sharp blow to the back of her head. The ground rushed up at her and the world went black.

———

Leander McNelly walked into my office the next morning. I had been watching for an answer to my telegram and had felt pretty disappointed when nothing came in right away. Then, out of nowhere, he walked right into my office.

Boone was parked in a chair in front of my desk, bending my ear about Alice Brenham, the gentleman bandit and his lawman skills in general, when McNelly walked in.

I introduced Boone and told him the Texas Rangers were re-forming and that McNelly would be a captain for one unit.

Boone stood up, looked at McNelly and said "Dang." Then he offered his chair and went and got coffee for our visitor. The man could talk for hours about almost nothing, and that's all he had to say this morning when McNelly came in.

McNelly took a seat, and I filled him in from the top about the holdup in Kerrville, how the bandits had apparently come over to my county with the money after the robbery, and about my suspicions over the horses in the livery stable. I finished up telling him about Johnny Carr.

He sat listening without interrupting me until I finished. After setting his coffee cup on the desk, he got up and started walking around the office. He finished and sat down again.

"Glad you got holt of me," he said. "Sounds like this guy Carr might just be gettin' started, and we like to stop 'em before they get up a head of steam." He drummed his fingers on my desktop.

"Union army, you said...belt buckles on two others...mmm." He glanced over at Boone. "Have either of you," he asked, "heard of a place called No Man's Land?"

Boone shook his head.

"Heard of it," I said. "Piece of land Texas gave up some years back 'cause it had to if it was still gonna' be a slave-holding state." I glanced over to see McNelly nodding. "You think these guys are from No Man's Land?" I asked. "Seems like a long way to go to rob a bank or two."

"Yeah," McNelly agreed. "Long way to go, all right. Still, it's an outlaw's paradise up there, so they say. No law, nobody to chase 'em down. They can just hunker down and have a safe base in between holdups." He paused and stared at the wall. "Mostly, word is they rob folks coming down the Santa Fe Trail. Still, there's money in Texas, what with the cattle drives."

He shrugged. "Just thinkin' out loud, mostly. When an outlaw shows up in Texas I've never heard of, I start wonderin' where he comes from." He stood up and put his hat on. "Why don't we go over and look around at that livery stable?" he suggested.

The door slammed and Ike Hawkins came in, thumping along on his cane and looking more upset than I'd seen him in a long time. "Julia and Pete are both gone!" he blurted. "They both left yesterday afternoon, and we ain't seen neither of 'em since."

I froze with my hat halfway to my head. "They weren't at home last night?" I said, realizing as I said it that's what Ike had just gotten done telling me. "Did they say anything about going somewhere?"

He shook his head, then stopped. "Pete didn't say nuthin'," he said. "Julia told Jeanne she might stay in town, but I checked at the boarding house and the café, and nobody's seen either of 'em." He looked from me to McNelly. "Ain't never happened before," he told McNelly.

I walked past the desk, put my arm around Ike, and walked him to the door. "I won't rest until I've found 'em both," I told him. "You know there's nothin' more important to me. Best thing you can do is go home and be with Jeanne and Isaac. You hear anything more, you come tell me."

Ike nodded miserably, clapped his hat on his head, and stumped over to his buggy. I watched as he drove down the street.

McNelly came out, followed by Boone. "I'm still thinking the first place to check is the livery stable, don't you?" he asked.

I mounted up. "Let's go," I told him.

Elmer wasn't there, which made me even more worried than I already was. A quick look around told me neither Elmer's horse nor Carr's black gelding were there. A kid came out from one of the stalls, wiping his hands on his pants. I'd seen him around town, but I couldn't remember his name.

"Elmer's not around?" I asked.

He shook his head. "No. He asked me to watch things here, feed 'em, and clean out the stalls till he gets back. Said he'd pay me two dollars if I done it right." He folded his hands behind his back and stared nervously at the three of us.

"What's your name?" I asked.

"Newt." He didn't give a last name, but I didn't figure it mattered. He was just here for the two dollars.

"What time did Elmer leave?"

"Yestiddy, maybe mid-afternoon," he answered. He took off his hat and fumbled with it nervously.

"Anybody go with Elmer?"

He nodded. "Pete Hawkins went. I knowed him from around town. And somebody else I never seen. The three of 'em went out together."

"And a girl?" I asked anxiously. "Julia Hawkins? You know her?"

He shook his head first from side to side, then up and down. "What I mean is, I know her, but she wasn't with 'em. I ain't seen her around here."

I looked over at McNelly in frustration. "Did they say where they were goin'?" he asked.

Newt shook his head again. "They didn't say nuthin' about that," he said. He watched as we rode out, then went back to cleaning the stalls.

———

By the time Wagon and Harris rode into Waco, Wagon knew he needed to get Harris to a doctor. The shotgun pellets in Harris's arm were still in there, and Wagon was no doctor, but even he could see the wound was festering.

Wagon left Harris slumped over his horse outside the café while he went inside to ask about a doctor. A man stopped on his way out the door to point Wagon to the next block south on Main Street. A right turn at the corner, he told Wagon, would bring him to a doctor.

Wagon sat in a small waiting room while Harris disappeared inside. Wagon could hear the occasional moans and yelps. Half an hour later, Harris came out with a bandage around his arm and shoulder. Wagon walked over to pay the doctor, who looked at Harris suspiciously.

"How'd he get all those pellets in his arm?" the doctor asked.

"Hunting accident," Wagon told him, handing over the money.

"Mmmph." The doctor shoved the money into a drawer and walked away, talking to himself. "Lot of accidents in this town lately," he told himself.

They mounted up and Wagon led the way north of town, looking for the adobe hut Carr had told him about. Slowing his pace once he'd left town behind, he kept an eye peeled to his right. He found the hut right about where Carr said it would be.

Feeling pleased with himself, Wagon dismounted and walked toward the hut, but a foul smell stopped him in his tracks while he was still several yards away. Screwing up his nerve, he pulled his shirttail over his mouth and nose and pushed the door open.

Wagon retreated and bent over his knees at a safe distance outside, fighting the urge to gag.

"What?" Harris asked, still on his horse and several yards away.

"Dead body," Wagon answered. He led his horse into the trees about thirty yards deeper off the road. "Let's set up camp out here for a couple days," he said. "I got to get rid of that body and let the smell go away."

Leaving Harris in the trees, Wagon rode back into town and got them some food and supplies, including a shovel. As he stepped out of the general store, he saw a familiar face coming out of a door across the road. He stopped, searching his memory. Where had he seen that kid?

The café, back in Hico! It came to him suddenly. That kid had brought them their food at the café. Wagon stopped, watching the kid mount his horse and ride away. Why would a kid from Hico be here? Wagon's eyes traveled up to the sign on the door across the road. The words on the door jumped out at him. It was the county jail and sheriff's office.

Wagon pulled his hat down over his eyes, loaded the food on his horse, and climbed up, pushing a shovel into the rifle scabbard on the saddle. He moved out slowly, riding out of town and breathing a sigh of relief as he left Waco behind.

He knew Harris would want to make the trips to the café, looking for Carr every morning. Wagon would just let him do that. After all, Wagon still had to pull that dead guy out of the hut and bury him. That was enough. Harris could take the chance of being caught by the sheriff for that robbery in Hico.

————

Lieutenant Pike Hardy was ordinarily a patient man. Level-headed, that's another word they often used to describe him. That was one of the reasons they had assigned Lieutenant Hardy and his command to the area they had to cover.

There was a short stretch of the Santa Fe Trail, right after it left Kansas and right before it reached the New Mexico territory. That short stretch of the trail dipped down into No Man's Land. It was generally called the Cimarron Cutoff. That was the part that gave Hardy and his troops the most trouble. It was three day's hard ride from Fort Union in New Mexico, and even farther from Fort Larned in Kansas.

Folks had thought the hardest part would be to

protect the settlers and their wagons and livestock from the Comanches or other Indians that might still raid the wagons. That hadn't turned out to be the case. It was the outlaws who hid out in No Man's Land. Those were the ones that made Hardy's blood boil.

Hardy looked at the man lying in the back of his wagon, muttering feverishly. They had shot him through the leg while he was trying to protect his family. Hardy looked over the back of the wagon at the wife and two small daughters. He had to ask, even though he knew the answer.

"What happened, ma'am?" he asked, trying to keep the rage out of his voice.

"One man came out of nowhere," she said, her voice catching as she spoke.

That was a surprise to Hardy. "Just one man?" he asked.

"Just one. When we had to stop, we fell behind the other wagons while we repaired a wheel. We were at the back. We weren't supposed to be, but one of the girls ran off this morning, and by the time we were ready to go—"

"Yes, ma'am," Hardy said. He didn't need to know why they were at the back, they just were. The outlaws always picked on the stragglers. "How did your husband get shot?" he asked.

"He was trying to protect me...this man grabbed me and..." She broke down in tears and Hardy stopped her.

"It's okay, ma'am," he assured her. "My men and I will stay with you until you catch up with the train, and we'll get your husband to a doctor in Fort Union. One of the men has some training as a medic, he'll help your husband until then."

Hardy jumped down from the wagon and stared off into the distance. "This one man, where did he go?"

The woman pointed vaguely to the south and east. "Off that direction," she said. "He just rode that way until he disappeared."

Hardy assisted the woman as she climbed up next to her husband in the back of the wagon. He assigned one of his men to drive the wagon while the wife stayed in the back. He stood staring off to the southeast, slapping one of his gloves into his hand. One of these days, he promised himself, he would convince his captain to let him take some men in there and clean out No Man's Land. That was the only way to put a stop to this.

CHAPTER 14

LEAVING A TRAIL

Julia moaned and rolled to her side, reaching with her hand to explore the pounding pain in her head. She touched a lump almost the size of an egg on the back of her head, moaning as she struggled to push herself to a sitting position.

"Ssshh!"

Julia stopped halfway up from the ground and looked to her left, where she had heard the hissing noise. Pete was sitting up, propped against a tree trunk. He was pressing down on his right shoulder. His eyes were a little bright with pain, but he looked awake and alert.

She looked around her. Men were scrambling in and out of the wrecked train cars. Passengers were lined up beside the train, dropping jewels and wallets into a bag being carried down the line by one of the robbers.

Julia struggled to her hands and knees to enable herself to crawl close enough to whisper to Pete. The movement cost her dearly and she struggled to suppress another groan.

"That's what this was about? Just robbing passengers?

This big of a train wreck, all for this?" Julia could hear the indignant tone in her own voice. "Are all these passengers rich or something?"

"I don't think so," Pete whispered back. "They've been scrambling in and out of one of the baggage cars down there." He pointed, then dropped his hand quickly, his eyes closed against the pain.

Julia leaned over, lifted his hand away, and looked at Pete's shoulder. A bullet had cut a deep furrow across the top of his right shoulder. Julia tore off the bottom of one of her sleeves and packed it down over the wound. She then tore off the bottom of the other sleeve and wrapped it around Pete's shoulder, passing it under his armpit to hold down the bandage.

She leaned back and looked at the baggage car. Men were carrying wooden boxes out of the car and setting them on the ground. "What's in there?" she whispered.

"They opened the first box a while ago," Pete answered. "They have rifles in there. I'm guessing it's a shipment of the new Winchester '73 rifles." As he spoke, a man tore open a smaller box and lifted out a large box. It appeared to be heavy. "And ammunition," Pete finished grimly.

"What's going on with you?" Julia asked abruptly. In her initial disorientation, she had forgotten about trailing Pete all the way out here, obviously a part of this gang of robbers. She turned to watch his face as he answered.

Pete's eyes dropped to the ground in embarrassment. "Elmer introduced me to this new guy in town, Johnny Carr," he mumbled. "Carr said I could make a little money on my day off sometimes. Said he was gathering cattle to drive to Kansas, and all I had to do was help hold the horses and gather the cows."

Pete could not lift his eyes to meet his sister's gaze. "The first job we went on, it turned out I was holding their horses while they robbed a bank over in Kerrville. Carr told me if I didn't keep working for him, or if I opened my mouth to anybody, he would kill my whole family."

Now he lifted his eyes to look at Julia, his expression was a little defiant. "So," he continued, "when I came with them this time, I brought a gun. I was determined not to help them pull off another robbery. I guess," he finished lamely, "you got here just about in time to see how that turned out."

Shouts from one of the other baggage cars interrupted Pete's story. They turned and looked at the train—two men were hopping down from one car, holding a box up in the air and shouting.

"Now, what's that about?" Pete wondered. He shook his head in frustration and shot a quick, embarrassed glance at his sister.

The anger and indignation drained out of Julia. She reached out to cover his hand with hers. "I thought it might be something like that," she said. "I never trusted that Elmer kid." She paused and gave Pete's hand a squeeze. "I'm here now," she reminded him. "We'll work together.

"They could have killed us both," Julia continued, thinking out loud. "I wonder why they didn't."

"I think," Pete said, "It's because you are Jake's...uh, girlfriend, and I'm your brother. They think maybe they can get Jake to do some things...or not do some things, if they are holding us."

"Ohhh." Julia turned that one over in her mind, wondering how they were going to get out of this. She looked up to see one of the robbers coming in their direction. "Is that Johnny Carr?" she whispered, sliding back down to the ground.

Pete nodded.

"Maybe," Julia said, "it's better if he doesn't know I've come around yet." She closed her eyes and waited.

———————

Carr bent down and picked up one rifle from the first box. He worked the lever a couple times and sighted down the barrel, then decided this one was his. He turned and carried his old Henry rifle to the kid, Elmer.

"This is yours, kid," he said. "Now, I've got a job for you." He waved at the boxes his men were carrying from the train. "We need a wagon to haul this stuff." He shoved two dollars into Elmer's hand. "Get into Austin and rent a horse and wagon to haul this stuff. Get back as fast as you can."

Elmer took the money and looked around, clearly bewildered. "Follow the tracks, dummy," Carr yelled. "The tracks will take you to Austin."

Shouting from a baggage car irritated him further. Carr turned on his heel and stalked toward the yelling. Two of his men jumped from a car, holding the box in the air and yelling.

"What?" Carr barked. "What are you yelling about?"

The men lowered the box and Carr looked inside. There was cash. A lot of it. Paper, mostly, but a few gold coins, too. "How much?" he breathed.

Both men broke into a grin. "About two thousand. Mebbe a little more," Blondie said. "We didn't count it all."

Carr picked up the lid from the box and read the paper tacked onto it. This shipment was going to the same place as the Winchester rifles. Payroll, he thought. It must be payroll for the new Texas Rangers. A grin spread across his face. Nice of the Rangers to help pay for his setup at the Roost.

Carr turned and strode toward the kid Pete and McCabe's girlfriend, over in the trees. As he walked, Jamison called his name and trotted over to walk with him. "How we gonna haul this stuff to Waco?" he asked.

Carr waved a hand to dismiss him. "I sent the red-haired kid to Austin to get us a horse and buggy," he answered. "The kid can haul 'em in the wagon for us."

Carr reached Pete, leaning back against a tree. The girl was still lying on the ground, not moving. Carr frowned. "If your sister don't wake up in the next few minutes, it'll be your job to wake her up and get her ready to move," he snarled. "You ain't stayin' behind, and you ain't gonna hold us up. Make sure she knows." With that, he turned and strode away.

———

Julia opened her eyes slowly and focused on the retreating back of Johnny Carr. She pushed herself up to one elbow when Carr reached the train and boarded one of the baggage cars. Pete turned to look at her.

"Did you hear him?" he asked. "He's taking us with him." He paused and adjusted the bandage over his shoulder. "I thought he was gonna kill us," he blurted. "Do you think he knows you killed that one guy? Beard, that's what they called him."

"He probably knows," she answered. "He's going to

take us with him to keep Jake from killing him. Plus, I doubt he cared about losing Beard." She paused and thought about what she had heard. "That other guy came over to Carr and said something about going to Waco, didn't he?"

"He did." Pete watched as the men pushed the passengers back into two of the cars behind the engine. Thankfully, none of the passenger cars had been derailed. He turned back to look at his sister. "What are you thinking?"

"I'm thinking we need to help Jake find us," she answered. "He'll be looking when we don't come home, and he'll hear about robbers striking this train. He'll be out here trying to put the pieces of the puzzle together."

Julia fingered the scarf she had in her pocket. Jake had given it to her on her birthday last winter. She had stuffed it into her saddlebag yesterday and had taken it out and wrapped it around her neck when it got a little cool last night. This morning, in a hurry, she had simply stuffed it in her pocket before she rode out.

She looked around her. They were in a stand of live oak trees, but ten yards to her left and down the hill a little, the live oaks gave way to scraggly mesquite trees and thick underbrush. She rose to her knees and looked over her shoulder. The outlaws were preoccupied with searching the baggage cars and herding passengers back onto the train.

"I'm going over there," she said, pointing at the mesquite and underbrush, "to leave a clue for Jake. Let me know if they come back this way."

Staying on her knees, she crawled to the mesquite, picking up a stick along the way. When she reached the underbrush, she moved around to the back side of it and tied her scarf onto two of the small, low-hanging branches she found. Underneath, she used the stick to write a simple message, digging the letters deep.

The message simply said, "Waco."

Crawling back to the oak trees, she picked up her pace when she saw Johnny Carr jump out of a baggage car. She covered the last three yards on her belly, staying out of his line of view. When he climbed the hill, he found both Julia and Pete leaning up against a tree.

"You came around," Carr observed gruffly. "On your feet and on your horses. You're coming with us, just in case that boyfriend of yours gets any ideas."

Carr grabbed her arm and steered Julia toward her horse. She pretended to stumble when she tried to mount. She reasoned that if Carr thought she was weaker than she actually was, it might give her an advantage somewhere along the way.

Carr shoved her roughly up onto the horse. "You better keep up, sister," he growled, then grabbed the reins of both their horses and led them down to join the others, who were now mounted and waiting.

———

Boone and I split up, checking every place in town where somebody might have seen Julia or Pete in the last day. While we checked, McNelly went to the telegraph office. He said he would send telegrams to Austin, San Antonio, and Waco asking if there had been any robberies at banks, any train holdups, anything to give us a place to start.

Two hours later, Boone and I had to give up. Nobody had seen either of them for several days. We rode back out to the livery stables, the last place we knew where they had been. The kid Newt wasn't any more helpful than he'd been before, except to say *maybe he'd seen 'em ride down and take the trail off thataway*, pointing east.

Well, that was something we didn't have before. The trail to Austin was down the road a bit from the livery stable. Boone and I rode down to it, dismounted, and studied the trail. There had been too much traffic in the day since Julia and Pete would have ridden out to give us much confidence we could track them.

"We could just ride that way an' see what we see," Boone suggested, staring down the trail.

"Might be all we got," I agreed, "but let's go back and find McNelly first. Maybe he's got something from those telegrams."

———

McNelly was back in my office when we returned. He had two sheets of paper in his hand. Sitting in a chair near McNelly was Isaac Hawkins, little brother to Julia and Pete. He stood when we came in, twisting his hat in his hands.

"Ma and Pa, they're worried sick," he said. "They sent me into town to find out if'n there's anything you can tell 'em."

"Hang around for a minute," I told him. "Maybe we'll have somethin' you can tell them."

McNelly walked around the desk and handed me one of the telegrams:

> *No bank robberies or holdups.*
> *Train from Houston didn't arrive.*

Carrying Winchesters and payroll.

I didn't recognize the name below the message. I gave it back to McNelly.

"Came from Austin?" I asked.

"Yup. Came from Rangers headquarters, which is just gettin' set up. New Winchester '73 rifles and first payroll for the new Rangers until we finish getting set up and running there in Austin. Sounds like a mighty big target for this guy Carr."

He handed me the other message. It came from the sheriff in Waco, saying there had been a holdup in Hico, two days ago. I gave it back.

"Couldn't be Carr, not up that far north just two days ago," I said. "But we think maybe Carr went east when he left here. He could have ridden pretty much all night and stopped that train, maybe up close to Austin."

"That's what I think," McNelly agreed. He put on his hat and picked up his Winchester. "You boys ready to ride?"

I patted Isaac on the shoulder. "We might have something," I told Isaac. "Go on home, tell 'em what you've heard. We'll be gone for probably a few days, but I won't rest till I find 'em."

We stopped off at the café to get some food for the trail, then got all the ammunition we might need over at the general store. We were on the trail to Austin thirty minutes later.

———

Pushing through the night with just a few stops to rest and water the horses, plus a one-hour stop for a little shuteye for the three of us, put us into Austin at mid-morning the next day. We went straight to the train station, where McNelly introduced us to another Texas Ranger named Trey Stanton.

Stanton told us he had ridden with another man to the site of a train wreck yesterday afternoon. When the train was over two hours late, the railroad people had notified the Rangers and the sheriff. Stanton told us there was no sign of the Winchester rifles or the payroll at the site of the crash.

Several of the passengers were there, waiting for another train. McNelly brought four of them over and asked me to describe Johnny Carr.

I realized there wasn't anything about Carr that really stood out. "About my height, maybe a little heavier," I said. "About thirty-five years old, rode a black gelding."

The passengers looked back and forth at each other. "Mebbe the guy in charge fits that description, one man said. "Guy walked around, barkin' orders at the others. Didn't see his hoss, though. They was all just walkin'."

The other passengers looked back and forth, nodding, agreeing I could have described the guy in charge, but it was hard to be sure. He looked like a lot of guys.

"A woman?" I asked. "Was there a woman with them, late twenties..." They all shook their heads at once. "Didn't see no woman," the man said. "They didn't have no woman with them."

I thumped one fist into my open hand in frustration. All I had was a possibility that Carr had staged the holdup, but they were sure there wasn't a woman with the outlaws.

I turned away, then turned back when another idea

hit me. "Was there a young guy, a kid, maybe twenty, with a headful of the reddest hair you've ever seen?"

All the heads went up and down this time. "Yup," said the same man who had been speaking for the group. "Flamin' red hair, it was. Couldn't miss it when he took his hat off. That was some red hair."

McNelly leaned in. "What else?" he said, his voice picking up a notch. "Did the kid do anything special, was he with another kid about his age?"

The heads shook back and forth in another no. "Don't remember nobody else that young," said the same man, who always seemed to answer for the others. "Just the one kid, holdin' hosses, mainly." He paused for a moment. "He left afore the others, though. The guy givin' orders told him to go do somethin', I guess. He jumped on his hoss and left early."

We asked a few more questions, but all they could tell us was that all of the robbers were gone when they left the site. The kid with the red hair had left first. They had seen little after that. The robbers had made them get back on the train and had tied bandanas over their eyes.

The railroad had sent down enough wagons to bring all the passengers, fifteen of them, up to Austin several hours later. They hadn't seen anything else unusual on the way up.

We backed away, and the three of us started talking.

"Had to be Elmer," I said. "Not too many folks have red hair that bright. No sign of Julia, though. Sounds like she wasn't with them."

"Maybe they just didn't see her," McNelly said. "They could have held Julia and Pete as prisoners over where the passengers couldn't see them." He stroked his chin and gazed at the floor. "They sent Elmer away early. I wonder why?"

Boone slapped his leg so hard it made me jump. "Wagon!" he shouted. "They needed a wagon to haul them boxes of rifles."

———

The second livery stable we found told us a kid with flaming red hair had rented a horse and wagon the day before, around noon. He had brought the wagon back the same night—last night.

"We've got to go down there," I said. "We've got to go down there where they stopped the train. I have to know if there's any sign of Julia and Pete down around the place where the train wrecked."

McNelly mounted his horse and reined it around. "Sounds like a plan," he said. "Let's see what we can find at the train wreck."

CHAPTER 15

WACO OR BUST

The train wreck site, when we reached it about an hour later, left me kinda stunned. None of the passengers had been killed, but we had seen broken bones here and there, up in Austin, plus a lot of bruises. There were a couple of docs in Austin who were pretty busy today. I realized now how lucky everybody on that train had been. It could have been a lot worse.

Off to one side, there was a line of derailed cars piled into a thick stand of live oak trees. Several trees had gone down before they stopped the cars. It looked like a tornado had gone through the place. The last baggage car plus the caboose were lying on their sides. No telling, I thought, how long it would be before the railroad could get this track open again.

We rode around the wrecked cars, knowing Trey Stanton, the Ranger from Austin, had already covered this ground, but we figured he might have been more concerned with getting injured passengers up to Austin.

After a while, we dismounted and started covering the ground on foot.

The first thing that got our attention was several wooden crates, lying on the ground near the baggage cars. Someone had pried them open and they were empty now. McNelly picked up one lid and poked around in the crates. He came over to us, shaking his head and scowling.

"They got the Winchester rifles, all right," he told us.

We all kicked around in the debris on the ground and prowled through the baggage cars we could get into. There was no sign of the payroll money, and more importantly to me, no clues that would tell me Julia and Pete had been here.

I approached McNelly and Boone as they jumped out of a baggage car. "Can I get your help with something?" I asked. Without waiting for an answer, I plowed on. "McNelly's right—if Julia and Pete were here and none of the passengers saw them, they woulda been held prisoner somewhere out of sight."

McNelly and Boone both nodded, already looking at the thick stands of trees around us. They knew where I was going with this.

"You wanna split up and look around in the trees and underbrush and such," Boone put in. "See if we can find any sign of 'em."

"Right." There was nothing else I needed to explain. We split up, with McNelly taking the east side of the tracks and me taking the west side. Figuring nobody had been waiting in front of the collision on the north side, Boone took the south.

I worked from about where the train had come around

the curve up to the barrier where the crash happened. I cast back and forth in the trees and brush on the west side. It didn't take long to find places where horses had been hobbled, based on tracks and droppings. There were also places that would have made pretty good cover for the outlaws waiting for the train. I saw nothing that made me think Julia would have been here, so I kept going.

I had just about come even with the engine, maybe twenty yards west of the tracks, when I found something that looked an awful lot like a shallow grave. My heart sunk. I stared at it, afraid to do what I needed to do.

Finally, I went and picked up one crate lid, then used it like a shovel. I dug slowly and carefully, tossing dirt away using the crate top. Boone saw what I was doing and came to help me. When the crate lid hit something solid, I tossed it aside and Boone and I started using our hands to brush away dirt.

After maybe two minutes, I uncovered a face. Relief flooded through me when I saw it wasn't Julia or Pete. This was somebody I'd never seen before. We kept brushing until we could see his face more clearly.

"Never seen 'em," Boone said.

I shook my head. "Me neither," I told him. "Let's keep going and see if we can tell how he died."

After another five minutes, that part was pretty clear. There was a gunshot wound in his chest.

Boone leaned over for a closer look, then turned his head to spit. "Plugged him dead center," he observed. "Nice shot from somebody."

I sat back on my heels to think things over. None of the passengers had said anything about hearing gunshots, but there had to have been a tremendous amount of noise, what with the crash, then cars derailing and running into the trees. No real surprise if they hadn't heard a gunshot or two.

But, considering this had to be one of the robbers, who had shot him? There could have been a falling out among thieves, or maybe Pete or Julia had gotten off a shot.

I stood and picked up the crate lid. "Let's cover him back over," I said. "Can't leave him out here for the buzzards."

"Don't know why not," Boone grumbled, but he grabbed the other lid and helped me. In another five minutes, I began moving farther over to the west.

After I'd covered twenty yards, I dropped to my heels, studying the ground. There were footprints, a lot of them. I figured there had been at least two people here and maybe three. Somebody wore a smaller boot and had left only a few prints.

My eyes traveled around, noting spots where somebody might have laid down in the leaves. Something caught my eyes, over by the trunk of a live oak tree. I reached out and picked it up—it was a thread. I stepped over and examined the tree trunk. There was a spot on the trunk where the bark was a little darker.

Taking out my knife, I dug out a little chunk of the bark, looked it over, and gave it a sniff. I handed it over to Boone, who did likewise.

"You thinkin' it's blood?" he asked.

"Maybe." I didn't want to think about it, but that seemed most likely.

I stepped back from the tree and tried to put myself in Julia's place, assuming she had been here. If she couldn't get away, she would try to leave a trail for me. How, I wondered, would she do that?

I looked around, trying to fight down the worry I felt inside that it was her blood or Pete's on that tree. If she had left a clue, she would have left it someplace where Carr and his gang wouldn't find it. Someplace deeper in the woods, in other words, farther away from the train. But if she'd been shot or hurt, she wouldn't be able to go very far.

I stepped out several yards to the west, away from the train, moved off to my right, and began walking a half-circle, coming back to the left. I passed Boone and the tree where I'd pried off the bark. Three steps later, I stopped in my tracks.

Something was trapped up against a mesquite tree over there, and it looked like cloth. I trotted over, bent down, and found the scarf I had given Julia last winter. I untied it from the tree, feeling the hope soaring inside me.

I glanced back down and immediately dropped to one knee, squinting and shielding my eyes from the afternoon sun. I broke into a grin and turned to holler at Boone. No need for that, it turned out. He was standing right behind me, looking over my shoulder.

"Waco," he said. He broke into a chuckle. "Smart girl, that one. I allus said it. That Julia is a smart girl. Cain't quite figger out why she took a shine to you, of course, but still, in all, she's a smart girl."

I ignored Boone, like I do most of the time, and stood up when I saw McNelly coming around the train engine, heading toward us. I waved my arms to flag him down.

"Got something?" he asked eagerly. I handed him the scarf and pointed at the word Julia had scrawled in the dirt.

McNelly squatted down to read the message in the

dirt, then looked at me, holding up the scarf. "This belongs to Julia?" he asked.

"It's the scarf I gave to her last winter," I told him.

McNelly stood and gave the scarf back to me. "Nothin' else for us here, far as I can tell," he said. "Looks like our next stop is Waco."

McNelly broke into a trot, heading for his horse. I moved to follow, but Boone held me back with a hand on my arm.

"You always said we're the law just in our own county," he reminded me. "You told me not to be tryin' to enforce the law outside our county. You okay with goin' to Waco? You ain't the law up there."

I looked at the scarf in my hand. "They took Julia," I said grimly. "Until I hunt down Johnny Carr, it's gonna be McCabe's law."

———————

The ride to Waco took three long days in the saddle. Julia was grateful for the fact the outlaws were hauling guns in a wagon—that had kept Carr from pushing them even harder. He had tried to make it in two days, but the wagon couldn't keep up.

Some of it was Carr's fault. Julia grinned when she thought about it, despite the seriousness of their situation. Carr had told Elmer to return the rented horse and wagon, then had gone to another livery stable and bought an old, beat-up wagon and a horse whose best days were long behind him. He'd had no intention of coming back with the rented wagon and he didn't want anybody coming after him because of that.

Carr wasn't willing to leave the guns behind, of

course, so they had taken the extra day, which had given Pete a little more rest. Three days after the train wreck, they reached the edge of Waco. Julia's headaches had mostly gone away. She was more worried about Pete than she was about herself. His wound wasn't festering, but he was feverish, tossing and mumbling in his sleep.

Carr called a halt when they got close to Waco, turning aside before they reached the big suspension bridge. They had backtracked and moved off the trail to find a place to pitch camp. Carr had ridden into town but ordered the others to set up a camp and had strictly forbidden the others to come with him.

Julia helped Pete get comfortable, and when the ones called Jamison and Blondie had ridden off into the woods, killed a deer, and brought back meat, she had cooked it. Elmer had mainly sulked and kept to himself. Listening to Jamison and Blondie grumbling among themselves, she wondered if they might have a confrontation with Carr that she could take advantage of.

Carr had returned late and left early in the morning, going by himself again. Jamison had walked out to Carr's horse with him, and Julia heard some sharp words and loud arguing. The talking quieted and Carr rode off, going to Waco again. Jamison came back to camp, but she heard him telling Blondie that Carr had agreed the two of them could go into town tonight.

Carr returned in a foul mood and said almost nothing the rest of the day. Elmer avoided eye contact with both Julia and Pete. Julia wondered if he felt guilty over what had happened. Maybe she could use that to her advantage.

After dark, Jamison and Blondie saddled up and left for town. Julia watched them leave, then saw Carr rise and start walking toward her. She felt a moment of sheer panic. She had nothing to defend herself with, and Pete was weak after three days of fever and pain.

To her relief, Carr said nothing, producing a rope that he used to tie her hands and feet. He did the same to Pete, then moved back to his bedroll, flopped down, and went to sleep. Julia tried to get Elmer's attention. He was seated by a small fire, whittling on a stick and staring at the sleeping form of Carr from time to time.

Julia tried calling Elmer's name in a loud whisper several times. If he could hear her, he gave no sign of it. Finally, she knew it was time to take a chance. She glanced over at the sleeping Carr, then raised her voice, hoping it wouldn't be enough to wake Carr.

"Elmer!"

She saw him jump, then stare at Carr, who didn't move. Finally, he dragged his eyes up to look at Julia. He looked back at Carr, then tiptoed over to squat down in front of Julia. He said nothing, waiting for her to talk. He stared at the ground.

Julia knew she might have just this one chance, and it might not last for long. "You have to help us," she whispered. "Pete and I wouldn't be in this mess if it weren't for you. Pete thought you were his friend, and he trusted you. Now look at us."

Elmer looked over at Pete, who had dozed off and was muttering feverishly. He raised his eyes for the first time to look at Julia.

"Nothin' I can do," he mumbled. "Carr will kill me if'n I try to help you."

"Give me something," Julia pleaded. "He won't leave us alive. Sooner or later, he's going to kill Pete and me. Can you live with that? Do you know what they do in

Texas to men who kill a woman? To men who even help kill a woman?"

Elmer winced. Carr rolled over and muttered in his sleep. Elmer froze and stared across the campfire until Carr resumed snoring. "Don't know what I can do to help," he protested. "I ain't gonna get myself kilt, helpin' you."

"My gun," Julia answered. "They took my gun after I shot Beard. Have you seen it? Where did they put it?"

Elmer backed off and shook his head.

"You know where it is, don't you?" Julia leaned forward, trying to make eye contact again. "Just get my gun and hide it in my bag over there." She angled her head to show her bag lying next to her. "Nobody will know you did it. Give Pete and me a chance."

Elmer swayed back and forth on his heels, mumbling to himself. Then he rose and went to the wagon, parked under some trees at the edge of the camp. He reached into the wagon and Julia heard soft rustling noises. Elmer returned, his hands behind his back, and Julia caught a brief glimpse of her gun as he stuffed it into her bag.

"Ain't got but one bullet in it," he muttered as he rose. "Don't know where your ammo is, and I ain't gonna look. You get one bullet." He stopped and stared at her. "You've gotta promise you ain't gonna shoot me."

Julia nodded. "I promise I won't shoot you."

Elmer fled back to the campfire, picked up his knife, and went back to whittling, humming nervously while he did.

Julia leaned back and let out a silent sigh of relief. A gun and one bullet were a lot more than she'd had a few minutes ago. She looked over at Pete, who had come awake. He managed a weak grin and a nod, then dozed back off.

———

Johnny Carr was up at daybreak, already in a foul mood because he was the only one up. Jamison and Blondie were snoring and sleeping like dead men. Carr could smell the whiskey from here. He walked over and gave each of them a kick. Elmer saw him coming and scrambled out of his blankets.

Growling because there was no coffee, Carr saddled up and yelled at Elmer.

"You! Kid! Untie the woman and the boy." He swung his horse around to face all of them. "Be ready to move out when I get back," he barked. He rode out of camp, struck the trail to town, and disappeared.

He had decided. Harris, Wood, and Wagon were supposed to meet him here in Waco. They had instructions to send one person to the café each morning to meet him. Nobody had come yesterday. Not that Carr didn't know where they were supposed to be—he knew exactly where the adobe hut on the north side of town was. The trouble was, he had left a dead body there. If the law had found it since he left, he didn't want to walk into a trap. He would let the others do that.

The problem was, he was carrying a load of fifty stolen Winchesters and a payroll. Both belonged to the Texas Rangers, and he didn't want to stick around if those guys were after him. He had to move out by tomorrow, whether or not Harris, Wagon, and Wood showed up. If nobody showed today, he would take his chances and move camp to the adobe hut, get supplies in town today, and light a shuck for the Roost by tomorrow.

Reaching the café in town, Carr ordered some breakfast and took a seat near the window after scanning the room. None of his three men were in here. Carr took his coffee and sipped, nearly scalding his tongue on the hot liquid. He swore bitterly and slammed the cup down, mumbling under his breath until the food arrived.

When his breakfast came, Carr dug into his bacon and eggs, wondering how long he would stay in the café, waiting for somebody to show up. He paused with a forkful halfway to his mouth when he saw a man ride in and dismount outside the café. The hat was pulled low, but it looked like Harris. Carr set his fork down and waited.

The man took a step toward the café, then looked past the café and down the street. He pulled up short and turned his head away, then took a quick glance down the street again. This time, he stepped back and pulled his hat even lower. After another quick look, he turned, remounted, and rode out in the direction he'd come from.

Carr shoveled down the rest of his food in two quick bites, threw a couple of coins on the table, and hurried out the door. He was pretty sure that was Harris. Why had he taken off like that?

Bursting out through the door, he nearly ran a man over just outside the café. Carr threw out an elbow and prepared to launch a fresh round of cursing until his eyes focused in on a star resting on the man's chest. Sheriff's badge—the realization hit him instantly.

Carr mumbled an apology and backed away. The sheriff flicked a brief glance at Carr, then went back to staring down the street. Carr stepped over to untie his horse, swung aboard, and left town in the opposite direction from the way Harris had left, if in fact that was Harris.

The thing was, Carr was pretty sure it was Harris. The question was, why was Harris so nervous about being seen by the sheriff? Why did the sheriff seem to be so interested? Carr needed to move his men around Waco, check the adobe hut, and see what was happening with Harris and the others.

CHAPTER 16

ABANDONED

Johnny Carr made the return trip to his temporary camp, his mind still trying to make sense of what he had seen in Waco. Harris should have arrived in Waco with the others only two days ago. Had he attracted the sheriff's attention in two days? How?

His crew was ready to go when he got back to the camp. It improved his mood for only about two minutes. He rode over to talk to Blondie, who he figured knew this area better than the rest of them.

"Do you know a trail around Waco?" he asked abruptly.

Blondie pulled back, still trying to quiet the pounding in his head. He'd heard the words, he just couldn't make sense of them right away. "Around?" he mumbled.

Carr leaned over to put his face two inches away from Blondie's face. "Around!" he roared. "You don't think I'm gonna haul a wagon full of stolen rifles through the middle of town, do you?"

Blondie recoiled from both the shouting and the smell of Carr's breath. He felt the bile rising in his throat and saw the red flush creeping up Carr's cheeks. He wasn't really sure if he knew of a trail, but he had a vague memory of one, and he didn't dare say no.

"Sure, there's a trail," Blondie said, sounding more confident than he felt. He didn't want to wander around looking for one with Carr breathing down his neck. His brain scrambled for what to say.

"Can you give me, uh, thirty minutes to scout it out? I need to make sure it's safe before we take the guns and prisoners and such."

Chafing at the delay, Carr turned that one around in his head a few times, but it made sense. If the sheriff was onto Harris, Wood, and Wagon, he needed to let Blondie walk into it, not him. He nodded grudgingly. "Thirty minutes," he growled.

Blondie rode out without another word. He struck the trail north, going slowly, keeping his eyes peeled on both sides of the main road. He needed something just wide enough for the wagon to pass through. Five minutes later, he saw what he was looking for.

A narrow trail branched off to the left, snaking through the woods. It was narrow, but wide enough for the wagon. He followed it for ten minutes—that's all the time he had before he needed to turn around and go back. At the end of that time, he felt confident the trail branched around Waco. It made sense that others in the past had wanted to avoid town, and had left a trail. Maybe for the same reasons Carr and his gang were avoiding the town.

Blondie returned to the camp and gave Carr the nod. "Got a trail," he said, avoiding Carr's hostile stare. "It'll get us past Waco." He turned and waited for the others to fall in behind him, then led the way out.

Julia rubbed her wrists and ankles to get the blood flowing, then had just a few minutes to do the same for Pete before Carr ordered them to mount up. She gave Pete a hand, then climbed aboard herself, telling Pete to ride in front of her. He nodded and moved out. He was hanging on to his saddle horn, but he seemed steady.

Julia knew, without turning around, that Elmer was following her with the wagon, and Jamison was bringing up the rear behind Elmer. She had no doubt Jamison would follow through on orders to shoot them if she and Pete made a run for it.

They broke from the main trail after a few minutes of riding north, and it seemed obvious they were following a side trail around town. After about thirty or forty minutes, the trail forked right and rejoined the main trail. She assumed they were north of Waco now. Carr called a halt, then rode alone, going south, toward Waco. Julia watched him go, puzzled.

Carr wasn't sure if the adobe hut was north or south of where they had joined the trail, but his instincts told him it was south. He ordered a halt while he went to look. Nobody else knew what they were looking for, so this had to be his job.

He rode slowly, concentrating on the eastern side of the trail, that's where it would be if he was correct in riding south. Three cowboys passed him, riding north. Carr pulled his hat low and waved as they passed.

The trees thinned, and he saw the hut. He grunted in

satisfaction as he rode up to it, dismounted, and stuck his head through the door. Harris was sprawled on a cot, snoring.

Carr kicked the cot and stood back while Harris thrashed off the bed and got up, looking around wildly for his gun.

"It's me. Carr." Carr's voice stopped Harris in his tracks.

Harris straightened and turned. The relief on his face faded when he saw the hostile stare he was getting. "Hey, boss," he mumbled. "We didn't know you was in town yet. Didn't, uh, didn't see you at the café."

"I was at the café this mornin'," Carr snarled. "Saw you for just a minute. You left like your boots was on fire when the sheriff showed up." Another thought struck him and he looked around. "Where's Wood and Wagon?" he demanded.

"Wagon went to get us some water," Harris said. "There's a stream over yonder..." His voice trailed away when he looked at Carr's face. "Wood ain't here. He's, uh...well, Wood is dead."

Carr's jaw dropped, and he stepped in closer. Harris backed away and came up short against the cot.

"How?" Carr asked in a low, menacing tone. "How is Wood dead?"

"It were an accident," Harris started. "A terrible accident, back up the road in Hico."

Carr drew his Colt, cocked the hammer, and held the barrel against Harris's temple. "What kind of accident?" he growled. "What were you doing in Hico?"

Harris grew pale and felt himself fighting for breath. "A holdup. It was Wagon's idea, his idea all the way. He said we could hold up a general store where they kept a lot of money. They did, too, but the folks in town started shootin'. Wood got blowed away with a shotgun."

Carr left the Colt up against Harris's temple, staring and watching the man sweat. "Did you take off this mornin' because you thought the sheriff knew about it?" he demanded. "You think he's got you connected to the robbery?"

Harris gulped loudly and nodded his head up and down. "Don't know how he could know, but he seemed mighty interested in me this mornin', so I skedaddled."

Carr slowly lowered the hammer on his Colt and returned it to the holster. He stared thoughtfully at Harris's face, enjoying the sight of nervous sweat pouring down and dripping on the man's shirt. Harris wasn't all that useful, but on the other hand, Carr didn't know Wagon at all. He would have to sacrifice Wagon. And that kid Elmer. And the girl and the kid.

He had to figure all that out. Carr turned without another word, walked out, and re-mounted. He would bring the others to the adobe hut for maybe another day or two before going to the Roost. Well, he corrected himself, some of them would go to the Roost.

———

We had two very hard days of riding to reach Waco, riding into town at dusk and looking for the sheriff's office and a place to eat, in that order. McNelly had received a telegram from Sheriff Waters, telling him about a holdup in Hico. We had decided those weren't our boys, but it still seemed like a visit to the sheriff might still be worth it.

We rode down Main Street, checking the names above

the shops and stores as we rode. McNelly was in the lead, and he pulled in right after we passed the post office. It was the jail and the sheriff's office, according to the sign. We knocked and pushed open the door. A lean, no-nonsense-looking man of about fifty was parked behind the desk. He swung his feet down and stood up when he saw the badges.

"Fred Waters," he said as he checked McNelly's badge and shook hands. "Are you Leander McNelly, by any chance?"

"Guilty," McNelly said with a grin. He turned and introduced Boone and me. Waters pulled a couple extra chairs over and told us all to have a seat.

"Let me make another guess," he said, lighting a cigar, leaning back, and squinting through the smoke. "You're after the guys who wrecked the train south of Austin. Lookin' for those boys who took Winchester rifles belonging to the Rangers."

"Two good guesses in a row," McNelly rasped. "I don't believe I'll be playin' any poker with you, Waters."

Waters grinned. "Suit yourself, Captain," he grinned. "I love a good game of poker." He moved his gaze to me. "Where are you servin' as the sheriff?" he asked me.

"Gillespie County," I said. "We live in Fredericksburg." I could see the question coming, so I jumped and answered it upfront. "They didn't just take rifles," I said grimly. "They took my fiancée and her brother."

Waters put his cigar on a tray on the desk and leaned forward, his eyes narrowing. "Well now," he said, "that makes it different, don't it? What exactly can I do for you boys?"

McNelly laid out what we had seen at the train wreck. He filled Waters in about the payroll theft, as well as the

Winchester rifles. He finished up by telling Waters about finding Julia's scarf and the note she scratched in the dirt.

Waters cast a sympathetic look in my direction and fiddled with the cigar while he thought. "Well," he said, "I don't know if this has anything to do with the train robbery, but I think it might just be possible that the gang that held up the general store in Hico might be here in Waco. Mebbe one of 'em, anyway. Do you suppose Carr could be meetin' up with some others from his gang here in Waco?"

McNelly and I exchanged a look. "Best clue we've got right now," I told him.

"What've you got?" McNelly asked.

Waters told us he had seen somebody getting ready to go into the café this morning. One description he'd gotten from a kid in Hico—the one who reported the robberies, Waters explained—might have fit the guy he saw. When Waters had moved toward the café to get a better look, the guy had mounted up and taken off.

After he collided with somebody coming out of the café, Waters explained, then had taken the time to get his horse saddled up and moving, he'd lost the guy. "Rode north out of town, that's all I know," he explained. "I thought maybe he would show up again, and I'll be on the lookout."

McNelly turned around and looked out the window. "Getting dark outside," he observed. He looked at me. "I'll leave it up to you," he said. "Your fiancée. Wanna look now or wait until morning to look around north of town?"

"Too easy to get shot, riding up to somebody's camp in the dark," I said, fighting down my instinct to go now. "Better if we wait until morning."

"First light, I'll be pleased to show you around out there myself," Waters said. He stood up. "If you boys need food and a bed for tonight, I'll get you fixed up."

Carr stalked around the small clearing where the adobe hut was located. He directed Jamison to put Julia and Pete in the hut, then posted Blondie as the lookout. "No need to tie 'em up now," he said. "Tie 'em when it gets dark. Can't have 'em sneaking off into town."

After an hour of waiting, Wagon came back into the clearing, carrying several waterskins. He dropped them on the ground and looked around in surprise when he saw the newcomers. His expression turned to worry when he saw Carr coming out of the oak trees behind the hut, headed his way.

Carr stopped in front of Wagon. "Tell me about the holdup," he stated. He stared, unblinking, while Wagon talked about the disastrous holdup in Hico. Wagon noticed how Carr dropped his hands down to hook his thumbs in his gunbelt while Wagon talked.

Carr changed subjects without taking his gaze away from Wagon's face. "Harris, over there," he said, jerking a thumb in Harris's direction, "says he thinks the sheriff taken an interest in him when he was in town today. You know any reason why that would be?"

Wagon shook his head back and forth until he saw Carr's right hand move toward his Colt. Wagon stopped and gulped nervously.

"Kid from the holdup in Hico," he quavered. "Kid that brung our food to us in the café there. He was in town, talkin' to the sheriff."

Carr's eyes widened in surprise. This was worse than he thought. His first idea was to pull his pistol and kill Wagon on the spot, but he might still have a use for Wagon. Carr hated waste.

Carr pointed at Blondie. "Go take his place," Carr grunted at Wagon. "Watch the girl and the boy." He turned and motioned for Blondie to follow him.

Moving back into the trees, Carr stared off to the north. "We'll have to get out of here, moving north, up to No Man's Land," he said abruptly. "You know this place well enough to get us outta here without leavin' tracks somebody could follow?"

Blondie didn't have to think for very long. "Brazos River," he said. "Cuts through town, we would've crossed that bridge to come into Waco. The river is off to the west of us now. Takes a turn north of town. We can foller the trail a little longer, then cut west to the river. I dunno if it's shallow enough to wade the horses across, but if'n it's not, we can still wade 'em on one side for a ways, then swim 'em across and climb out. Cover our tracks on the other side."

Carr kept staring. Blondie wondered if Carr had heard anything, then Carr nodded abruptly and turned on his heel. "First light," he snapped. "Get ready to lead us outta here at first light."

Carr still wasn't happy about the situation. His gut told him the law was looking for him. The Rangers weren't going to be happy about losing their rifles and payroll, McCabe would be ready to kill him if he caught Carr after taking the girl, and to top it off, the local sheriff might have tied him in with that botched holdup in Hico.

Carr skipped the venison cooked by the woman and gnawed on an old piece of jerky while he thought things out. He rolled in his blankets later, staring up at the stars. They couldn't take the woman with them to the Roost. And even he didn't risk killing a woman. Half the sheriffs and Rangers in Texas would be after him. Finally, he had an idea.

———

I was up and had Sherman saddled at daybreak. McNelly and Boone weren't far behind me, but we had to wait a little for Waters. He made up for it when he showed up with some biscuits, bacon, and coffee. We grabbed the vittles and mounted up.

Waters led us out of Waco, moving north. We had to go a little slow, since morning light was still a little hazy and we had to stop to check out a few clearings and possible hiding spots as we went. I figured more than an hour had passed since sunup when Waters, out in front, held up his hand.

We stopped, fanning out a little to either side of Waters, and I strained to identify a dark object sitting back from the trail in a small clearing. It looked like a little building of some kind.

———

Carr hustled back and forth in the dim gray dawn, barking orders in a low voice and kicking anybody who wasn't out of their blankets yet. When the red-haired kid started to put a harness on the old nag pulling the wagon, Carr told him to hold off. The kid looked confused, but Carr didn't feel like an explanation just yet.

Approaching the hut, he saw Wagon waving for

somebody to take his place guarding the hut while he went to saddle up. Carr decided now was as good a time as any to tell the lie he'd thought up last night. He motioned for Elmer to join them.

Carr waited for Elmer, then put a hand on each of their shoulders and looked 'em in the eye. He'd found that he was pretty good at lying, what with all the practice he'd had over the years.

"We need you boys to stay behind while we scout a way out of here," he said smoothly. "We've got to get a route where folks can't see that the girl and the wounded kid are with us." He turned to Elmer. "Plus, we've got to be sure we find a route the wagon can follow. Give us just a couple of hours, and we'll be back for you."

Carr stepped back and looked at the others, saddled and ready to ride. "Everybody grab a second Winchester," he said. "Plus some ammo. No tellin' what we might run into out there."

He trotted toward his horse, waving at the others to mount up. He hated leaving those extra Winchesters behind, but it was time to cut his losses. He'd already stuffed the payroll money into his saddlebag. All the water and most of the food in the camp was distributed on the other men's horses.

Nobody had asked questions. Everybody knew it was time to get out of here. Bad luck for Wagon and the kid to get left behind.

———

Wagon felt relief at first. Carr hadn't shot him for the holdup in Hico. He'd said they were coming back for him and the kid. He looked over at Elmer, who had rolled up in his blankets and gone back to sleep. Wagon shook his head and untied the two in the hut. Then he sat down outside and took up guard duty again.

Wagon himself dozed for an hour, waking up just long enough to shift his position. After a while, he got thirsty as the morning sun started to heat things up. Wagon stood, scratched himself, and walked around to the side of the hut where they had stored the water and food under a tarp.

He lifted the tarp and froze in his tracks. The water and food were gone. Carr had left him behind, saddled with the two prisoners and that kid, Elmer.

CHAPTER 17

AMBUSH

Wagon felt a sick, sinking feeling in his stomach. Carr and the others were going to run for that safe hideout up in No Man's Land. Something told him he would be shot on sight if he got out of this mess and showed up at the Roost. That's if he didn't get shot before that, hanging around here.

Wagon trotted over to the wagon and helped himself to one of the new rifles. He broke open a box of ammunition and loaded it, then lifted the Winchester and sighted down the barrel. The kid Elmer woke up enough to roll over and Wagon shook him roughly.

"Get up, kid," he growled. "They left us. Grab a gun and get over there to help guard the prisoners."

Wagon moved back past the hut. The woman was knocking on the door and asking if she could come out. Wagon shoved the door open on the way past. "Leave the kid in there and don't get out of my sight," he muttered.

Stepping past the hut, he halted in his tracks and stared out to the road. There were some dark shapes out there, and he had just enough light to recognize the shapes as three men on horseback. An early morning ray of sun broke through the clouds and Wagon caught the reflected glint off a badge. He sprinted to the woodpile he had built with Harris, just to the left of the cabin.

Pulling out a few small branches and chunks of wood, he created a hole in the woodpile, just enough to see the road. He worked the lever on the Winchester '73 and pushed the rifle barrel into the hole.

———

Julia stepped out through the doorway, standing outside and trying to forget the lingering stench in the hut. Two steps outside the doorway, she heard sudden movement from Wagon. She turned and watched him dive behind a woodpile.

Julia turned back and looked out toward the road. Three men were out there, on horseback. She didn't know who they were, but it didn't take long to realize that if Wagon was going to shoot at them, she needed to help the men on the road.

She rushed into the hut and searched through her bag, coming out with the pistol Elmer had given back to her yesterday. She checked to see if it was ready to fire her one and only bullet. She wasn't taking any chances.

Rushing out the door, she heard Wagon lever the Winchester and knew she was out of time. He would dry-gulch at least one of them by the time she could turn the corner and get off a shot at Wagon.

Julia lifted the pistol and fired a warning shot, then ran back into the hut and dove to the ground. When Pete rose halfway out of his blankets, she held him down. Wagon fired—that shot was too close to the hut to be anybody else. Then came several answering shots. Wagon fired again, several times. There was nothing she could do but keep her head down and wait it out. She had no more ammo. A run to the wagon for a rifle might cost her life.

———

I had been reaching for my field glasses, trying to get a better look at that building, when a shot rang out. I jerked up in surprise, then felt a sharp sting on my neck. I yanked my Winchester from the scabbard and dove flat-out on the ground. There was a small ditch at the side of the road, so I crawled into it.

Several shots whistled overhead. I looked for the others. Boone was down in the ditch, too, probably also pinned down by the fire from the clearing. McNelly had done a little better, he was down behind a log and looked like he might have a decent field of fire over there.

It was a bad idea to raise my head. That guy had seen me dive into the ditch while he was shooting at me. I pulled off my bandana, ran it over the spot where my neck stung—it came away bloody. I dropped my bandana and considered my situation. It seemed like my one advantage was the ditch. I didn't think he could see me down here.

I turned and started worming my way over to the right. I didn't dare raise up, and progress was slow, but I moved along for several yards and stayed down, waiting. The shooting paused, so I took a chance and peeked up above the ditch. The morning light made things a little clearer now. There was a brick building of some kind over there. Probably adobe, I thought. I wondered if Julia and Pete might be in that hut.

Looking left of the building, I saw a woodpile. It was likely he was hunkered down and shooting from there. He sent a few more searching shots our way, and I was pretty sure I was right about him shooting from the woodpile.

It seemed to me that I could fire a few ricochet shots off that brick and make things pretty hot for him. I lifted my Winchester a little and got my elbow under me, preparing to get up to a firing position. Boone saw what I was doing, grabbed a branch, and waved it in the air.

A shot tore the branch from Boone's hand immediately, but it gave me all the time I needed. I popped up to one knee and levered three quick shots off the adobe. There was a yelp of pain, then somebody ran out from behind the woodpile, shooting as he came. McNelly and I fired at the same time, and he dropped to the ground.

None of us were eager to move. We did not know how many of them were in there, but it sounded like at least four guys had been in on the train robbery, maybe more, according to the passengers. The silence after all the firing just a minute ago was eerie. I looked over at McNelly. He shrugged and stared into the clearing, just as uncertain as me.

Finally, we all moved forward on our knees at once, guns at the ready. It looked like a good fifty yards to the adobe hut, and I was prepared to cover all of it on my knees, expecting somebody to pop out of those woods and open fire.

We had gone only a few yards when I heard a voice—

I knew that voice! "Julia!" I shouted, risking gunfire that never came.

"Jake!" she shouted. "If the man at the woodpile is down, Elmer is the only other one here. The rest of them rode out more than an hour ago."

Elmer, by himself, didn't sound as scary to me as the others. We all rose to a crouch, coming in low with guns ready. "Stay where you are," I told Julia and waited while McNelly scouted behind the building. Boone stayed out front, swinging his rifle from side to side.

I stepped into the adobe hut, and Julia launched herself at me. I hung on and staggered back, smoothing her hair as she squeezed me, repeating my name over and over. Pete was on the floor when I looked down. He looked a little pale and his shoulder was bandaged, but he managed to grin at me.

Julia let go and gave me a long kiss before she stepped back, tears of relief and happiness streaming down her face. "I knew you'd come," she whispered. "I knew you'd come."

McNelly stepped into the cabin, and Julia recognized him from that night her family had brought him to dinner at their house. She had introduced us, and that seemed like a long time ago. "Captain," she said, "you have no idea how glad I am to see you guys."

"It was that scarf and the note you scratched on the ground," he told her. "That's what got us here."

Julia smiled and lifted her hand to my shoulder and neck. I winced when she touched the wound. "Just a scratch," I assured her. "Your warning shot saved my life. I jumped, and his shot missed me by just enough."

Julia rummaged around in her bag and came up with a bandage she tied around my neck. She stepped back, then stiffened. "Elmer!" she said. "Elmer is still around here somewhere." She stepped to the entrance of the hut and pointed. "Over by that wagon," she said, "the last time I saw him, anyway."

I stepped out and Boone came with me, advancing slowly toward a wagon at the edge of the clearing. Halfway there, I saw a rifle barrel, pointed at the sky with a white rag wrapped around it. The barrel and the white rag were both shaking.

"Come out of there, Elmer," I told him.

———

Carr let them go north on the road for several hundred yards before he ordered Blondie to cut over through the trees to find the Brazos River. Blondie had said the river would take them north and a little west from here, and that's what they needed. Carr would waste no time getting to No Man's Land and the Roost. The sooner they covered their tracks in the river, the better.

The trees and underbrush grew thicker the more they moved west. Carr slapped away branches and cursed under his breath, wondering now if he should have let Blondie keep going on the road until he found a better trail west.

Finally, Blondie turned in his saddle and pointed, they had reached the river. The four of them emerged from the trees and paused on the bank, letting the horses drink. Eager to cover his tracks, Carr told Blondie to stay in the lead. The river was too wide and deep to just wade the horses across, so Carr planned to wade on this side for at least a couple miles before swimming them across. After they emerged, they would use branches and whatever they could find to cover their tracks on the other side.

Blondie urged his horse into the water and began wading along the bank. Harris and Jamison followed him. Carr brought up the rear, scanning the woods behind and listening carefully before wading into the river. There seemed to be no pursuit.

Guiding his horse along near the bank, Carr paused when he heard a faint boom that he thought could be a gunshot. There was another immediately following the first. Carr reined in and concentrated on the shots. Several more booms followed the first two. He urged his horse on, following the others. It sounded like the law had arrived back at the adobe hut.

———

Elmer came out, hands in the air and trembling. All the fight seemed to be gone from him. I tied his hands and sat him down outside the hut, then walked over to join McNelly. He had turned the guy over we had shot at the woodpile so we could see his face. I stopped to take a careful look at him, then shook my head at McNelly.

"I never saw him either," McNelly said. We marched Elmer over to where the man lay.

"They called him Wagon," Elmer said. "I think he came from Austin or somewhere around there. Jamison knew those guys."

The name Jamison didn't ring a bell. I shot a questioning look over at McNelly, who wrinkled his brow and stared off into the woods. "Maybe I've heard of him," he said finally. "Couple of stage robberies or somethin' like that. Small time bandit."

"Who else?" I asked Elmer. "Who were the others?"

He stared at me sullenly, shaking his head and looking away.

"Do you know how much trouble you're in already?" I asked him. "Let's see here, you kidnapped a woman and her brother, staged a train robbery and robbed the train—"

"I didn't do all that," Elmer flared. "The others done it, mostly."

"I'm not too sure the judge is gonna see it that way," I told him. "You're pretty young to be swinging from a rope. You help us, maybe the judge will see it differently. I'll have a word with him myself if you need help."

I looked across at McNelly, who nodded.

"Sure," he said. "I'll put in a word for you, too."

Elmer blew out a long, miserable breath. "It was Carr, Johnny Carr, that organized it all. He talked me into helping an' fooled Pete into thinking that it wouldn't be nuthin' but rounding up cows and horses for a cattle drive."

Elmer stopped and looked at me, trying to read my face. "Keep goin'," I said. "You're doing pretty good so far."

"Carr knew Jamison from the Army," he said. "Jamison got Beard and Blondie, or whatever their real names are." He stopped and looked over at Julia. "Beard is the one she killed," he explained.

"Anyway," Elmer continued, "the four of 'em robbed the bank in Kerrville. Pete and I held the horses. Pete tried to leave, but I wouldn't let him. Carr said he would kill Pete's whole family if he didn't come along.

"That's about all," he said. "Except..."

"Except what?" I asked, leaning in to hear the rest of it.

"Jamison brought one other guy, Wagon." He stopped and pointed at the dead man on the ground. "Carr sent Wagon to get a couple other guys, somewhere up in No Man's Land."

I raised my eyebrows and looked over at McNelly, who nodded.

"How many guys did he bring back from there?" I prodded.

"Two more, but they tried a holdup or something and one of 'em got shot. Carr was pretty mad about that. I think that's why he left Wagon behind. I guess he didn't like me much, either. He left me behind, too." Elmer kicked at a rock, resentment written on his face.

"How many got away?" McNelly asked.

"Four," said Elmer. "Carr, Jamison, Blondie, and the one that come down from No Man's Land. I think they called him Harris. That's all of 'em."

Elmer seemed to have told us everything he knew. McNelly, Boone, Waters, and I walked away. McNelly rummaged around in the back of the wagon. "Forty-three rifles back here," he announced.

"So, they got away with seven," I said after doing some painful arithmetic in my head.

"No," McNelly said. He reached into the wagon and took out two of the Winchesters. He gave one to Boone and the other to Waters. "Seems like you boys need a good rifle," he told them. "Looks like the outlaws got away with nine."

Boone let out a whoop and a whistle. He held out the Winchester at arm's length, grinning from ear to ear. "If that don't beat all," he beamed. "Makes this dadgum trip worth it, don't it?"

Waters tugged at his hat and nodded at McNelly. "I'll put it to good use, captain," he promised. "What do you boys want to do now?"

I looked over at Julia and Pete. "I've got to get back to town and get him a doctor," I explained. "And those two need to get headed home as soon as they can go. Their family is worried sick."

McNelly patted Boone on the shoulder. "They've got a head start of more'n an hour," he observed. "Probly headed to No Man's Land as fast as they can get there, but mebbe Boone and I could track them as far as we can, and you can take Julia and Pete to Waco an' see 'em off." He looked at Waters. "Can you take that red-headed kid with you and lock him up?"

We slung the dead man across his horse and tied him down, helped Pete up into the saddle, tied Elmer to his saddle, and mounted up for the ride back to Waco. McNelly and Boone turned north.

"We'll track them for a while," McNelly said, "then we'll likely be back in Waco. If they've got any brains, they covered their tracks in the Brazos River, but we'll try."

———

I waited in a little lobby area at the doc's office in Waco. Julia went inside with Pete and the doctor. She came out about a half hour later. She was smiling, so I knew the news was going to be good.

She gave me a kiss and sat in my lap. "He'll be fine. The doc cleaned the wound and re-bandaged it. He said I did a good job of keeping it clean. He wants Pete to rest here for a day, maybe two, then I can take him home."

She leaned back to look into my eyes. "What are you going to do?" she asked. "Are you going to track those guys into No Man's Land?"

"It depends on McNelly," I told her. "I've got no authority outside my county, but McNelly does. If he wants to track Carr and his gang to No Man's Land, I'll go with him. And you know nobody's gonna keep Boone out of it."

"I know," she said. "It's what I expected." She stood and gave me a kiss when I stood up. "Do what you need to do," she said. "I'll be waiting for you at home."

When I got to the sheriff's office, Waters was just getting Elmer locked up in a cell. I leaned against the wall and watched, trying to think of anything else Elmer might be able to tell me. That's when he surprised me.

"You said you'd help me if'n I help you, right?" he said, holding onto the bars of his cell.

"That's right," I nodded. "You got somethin' else?"

"The hideout," Elmer said.

"You already said it's in No Man's Land," I reminded him, leaning forward. "What else do you know?"

"I don't know anything, but Wagon went up there," Elmer mumbled.

"Wagon's dead," I reminded him. "I don't think he can help."

"I seen Wagon tuck somethin' in his pocket after he talked to Carr and afore he left for No Man's Land," Elmer said. "I think he had hisself a map to get to the hideout."

I came away from the wall and straightened up, looking at Fred Waters. "I checked his pockets when I dropped him off to get buried," Waters said. "His pockets were empty."

I stood for a moment, staring at the floor. "Saddlebag," I murmured. I look at Waters again. "Where is his horse?"

Waters pointed toward the street. "Out there," he said, "tied up out front."

I left the jail at a dead run. Waters was right behind me.

CHAPTER 18

RIDING THE RAILS

I unbuckled Wagon's saddlebag and dug around inside. When that didn't go fast enough, I started chucking stuff out onto the ground. Mostly, he carried food. No wonder they started callin' him Wagon. I threw out some stale biscuits, some jerky, and something else that smelled awful. I also threw out a knife and some cartridges. That got me to the bottom. I reached in and fished around on the bottom and came out with a folded piece of paper.

I heard hoofbeats and looked up to see McNelly and Boone. They looked at the stuff on the ground, then at the paper in my hand.

"Lost them at the river, just like I thought," McNelly said. "No tellin' how far up the bank they waded or where they got out of the river. He pointed at the paper. "Whatchya got? Is that from Wagon's saddlebag?"

I unfolded the paper and took a good look. I passed it over for the others to see. "Looks like directions to Carr's hideout," I said. "Carr must have taken a train down here. Several trains. And there's a map to the hideout for the last part of the way."

McNelly stared at it for a long time. "Three trains," he noted. "The Houston and Central Texas to Dallas, then you switch to the KATY—The Missouri, Kansas, and Texas through The Nation to Topeka, Kansas. Then the Atchison, Topeka, and Santa Fe, west through Kansas. Says you get off that one at the end of the line, almost to Colorado."

McNelly moved to get the glare out of his eyes and squinted at the map at the bottom of the page. "Day's ride from there to his hideout. West corner of No Man's Land, right at the northern edge. Calls it the Roost."

McNelly passed the paper back to me and stared at the ground, stroking his mustache and thinking things over. Finally, I couldn't stand the silence.

"Do you think it's a real map?" I asked. "Not just something Carr put in there to throw us off the scent? Could we really get there on all those trains? And how long would it take?" I stopped to think things over. "I don't doubt he's got a hideout up there. Maybe that's really where it is."

"Well," McNelly said, still thinking things over. "I've taken the Houston and Texas Central, then the Katy to Kansas City. I guess it took about two days. The train don't have to rest, like a horse does, but you've got to stop for fuel, let the passengers stretch an' get food. Mebbe another day to the end of the Atchison, Topeka, and Santa Fe line. Day's ride to that Roost place. We could do it in five days, maybe six."

"Huh," I said, shaking my head. I hadn't ever ridden a train, but it sounded a lot faster to me. "I'm guessing you couldn't ride a horse up there inside ten or twelve days, not without killing the horse. Maybe if you swap for fresh horses several times, like the Pony Express, you could do it in a week."

"Or if you stop and steal horses," Boone put in. "Those boys wouldn't go around askin' folks an' being all nice about it."

Everybody stopped talking and watched McNelly. It was really up to him whether we did anything about this. He must have felt the eyes because he stopped staring at the ground and looked up at us. "Anybody wanna take a train ride?" he asked with a grin. "Those outlaw boys are going the wrong way to catch the train, and I'm thinkin' they don't want to be seen by nobody else right now. That means they're on horseback. We can meet 'em up there."

Boone beat me to it. "Can't think of a better way to break this baby in," he barked, waving his new Winchester '73 in the air. "This is why you gave it to me, I reckon."

"Me too," I said. "Count me in. I'll tell Julia where I'm going. Her dad, Ike, is an old campaigner. He'll hold the town together for me."

To my surprise, Waters threw his hat in, too. "I've got a deputy to watch things here," he told us. "I'll come with you boys. I like to finish what I start." He looked over at McNelly. "We can't catch the Houston and Central Texas line here. A spur line leads from here to a town called Bremond. We could catch the train there." He looked overhead at the sun. "Got to wait till tomorrow," he observed. "Only one train a day and that's gone."

McNelly looked around, grinning. "I'll deputize all you boys," he told us. "Proud to ride with you, I am." He stopped and stared at us thoughtfully. "Four of us," he mused, "an' four of them, plus probably a couple more at this Roost place."

He looked at Waters. "What time does the train leave tomorrow?" he asked.

"Ten o'clock sharp," came the answer.

McNelly patted Waters on the shoulder. "Show me to the telegraph office," he said. He looked around at the rest of us. "See you boys at nine-thirty in the mornin' at the train station."

Boone went looking for a room we could have at a boarding house tonight while I went back to the doc's office to see Julia. I found her sitting by Pete's bed. Pete looked perkier than he had a couple hours ago, I thought. It could have been the pretty nurse that was sponging off his wound.

Julia followed me outside, where I told her we planned to ride a few trains up to No Man's Land and finish what we started. I asked her to tell Ike I needed his help watchin' things back in town for me.

She didn't make any objections. She looked a little disappointed, maybe, but this was a strong woman who knew how things needed to be. "We can't let him do to anybody else what he did to Pete and me," she said. "You do what you have to do." She gave me a kiss, and we agreed to meet at the café for dinner.

———

Leander McNelly stood in the telegraph office with a pencil and a sheet of paper. He started to write his message, then threw that piece of paper away and started another. He started writing again, then stopped after a while to read his telegram.

*Pursuing outlaws who have robbed a train in
Texas.*
*Probably robbed settlers on the Santa Fe Trail
also. Stop*
*Have four men pursuing five or six men. They
have a*
*Rock fortress on a shelf of land, Northwestern
corner of*
No Man's Land. Stop
*Requesting detachment to help. Can meet at
Becknell, NM, in six days. Stop.*

Captain Leander McNelly, Texas Rangers

Satisfied, McNelly carried the message over and
handed it to the clerk. "I need to send this to Fort Union,
New Mexico Territory," he said. "Attention Captain
Alexander Wilson."

———

Alex Wilson had days when he wondered if it had been a
good idea to sign up with the Army after the war. He had
been a young man then, joining Grant's Army just before
the siege at Petersburg. The Army was a long way from
the cornfields of Iowa. His duty hadn't been hard, and
the war was over not long after he signed up. Then the
Army was short of men when the soldiers mustered out
after the war.

The idea of scouting the west, seeing unknown country, riding with the cavalry...well, it was a pretty exciting
idea to a twenty-year-old man. Now, eighteen years later,
he was a captain, but he had seen a lot of hard duty. Fort

Union wasn't a bad command, he had to admit. The worst was the grief he had taken from his superiors about not stopping the highwaymen working the Santa Fe Trail.

Wilson stared at the telegram in front of him. He didn't know a Captain McNelly, but he had certainly heard of the Texas Rangers, and this seemed like a good chance at stopping some of the outlaws on the trail. He knew who he wanted to send, the only question was how many men he could spare, and for how long? His troops were stretched thin already.

Wilson stood and opened his office door. His adjutant looked up from a rickety table in the room outside.

"Get me Pike Hardy," he commanded. "Right away."

The adjutant executed a smart salute and left. That's one thing, Wilson told himself. These men couldn't even give him a decent salute when he'd arrived three years ago. He had instilled good Army discipline in them. He would send his best man on this mission.

Lieutenant Pike Hardy appeared in the doorway, also executing a smart salute. Wilson looked up from his desk and liked what he saw: a young man, about twenty-five, tough as nails and smart as a whip.

"At ease, Hardy," Wilson said after returning the salute. He pointed at a battered old chair sitting by his desk. "Have a seat."

Hardy took the chair indicated, sitting ramrod-straight, his hat and gloves resting in his lap. Wilson passed the telegram across the desk. "Read it," he ordered.

Hardy scanned the telegram, then re-read it carefully. His head snapped up, his gaze at Wilson was intense. "Request permission to go, sir," he blurted.

Wilson waved his hand in the air. "Oh, you'll go," he

assured Hardy. "You'll lead the mission. I know you've been chasing these outlaws for a while. They always disappear somewhere into No Man's Land, and now is your chance. Tell me how many men you need and give me an estimate of how long you'll be gone. And tell me anything else you might need."

Hardy's head dropped as he read the telegram one more time. "Rock fortress on a shelf of land," he repeated to himself. He gazed at the top of Wilson's desk. "Probably got the high ground, five or six men," he murmured, again to himself.

His gaze traveled back up to hold Wilson's gaze. "Sir, I request six men. I expect it to take a week to ten days." He paused, then pointed out the window. "And I request Napoleon, sir."

Wilson's head swiveled around as he looked at an old twelve-pound Napoleon cannon, a relic of the war. Wilson couldn't remember using it in the three years he had been here. Then again, most of their action had involved chasing renegade Apaches, or robbers on the trail. Not a lot of call for a cannon for those missions.

Wilson swung back around and looked at Hardy doubtfully. "You want the cannon?" he asked, feeling a tad incredulous. "Napoleon? Does that thing still work?"

"It does, sir," came the quick and confident answer. "We have kept it in good condition, and I am certain it fires accurately." He paused. "One other thing, sir, I'll need Hostler to be one of the six men."

Wilson's doubtful expression came back, more pronounced than the first time. "Hostler?" He pictured a young private who'd come to them about a year ago. Skinny, always squinting to see things, had an Adam's apple that dominated his neck and bobbed up and down every time he swallowed. "You want Hostler? Why?"

"Hostler loves artillery, sir," came the quick answer. "Loves to work on Napoleon over there. Can make the old girl sing like a nightingale. Could pick a flea off a leaf with it. Sir." The last word came as an afterthought, and Wilson smothered the impulse to laugh.

"Okay, lieutenant, you can have six men, including Hostler, and you can have Napoleon. How long will it take you to reach Becknell?"

Hardy stared thoughtfully out the window. "What with hauling Napoleon, sir, I make it be four days, to be sure we get there on time."

Wilson nodded and stared back down at the telegram. "In that case, Lieutenant," Wilson said, "have your men briefed and ready to travel in two days' time. Good luck. That is all."

Hardy executed another salute and left without a word. Wilson could see the excitement in the young officer's eyes. He grinned briefly as he returned to the paperwork littering his desk. He could, he thought, use several more men like Hardy.

———————

Five days down the trail, Johnny Carr figured they might have only three more days to go. They had stolen fresh horses twice, but they had worn these down, and the farther north they pushed, the fewer places he could find to get fresh horses. He had pushed deep into the night twice, but the men and the horses had both had about what they could take.

Carr stared at the campfire and sipped at what was left of his whiskey. He knew about not staring at a campfire, but that's what his helpers were for—to keep a lookout. He had posted two men on watch after supper, but now they had come to the fire and arranged themselves around where he was sitting. Whatever this was, he knew it couldn't be good.

"What?" Carr barked so suddenly they all took a step backward. Best to carry the fight to them, he figured.

The three of them shuffled their feet awkwardly, then looked at Jamison to be their spokesman. He cleared his throat and stepped closer.

"We been on the trail for a while now, Johnny, pushin' hard," Jamison began. "We done stopped a train and robbed it, took a real chance kidnapping that girl and her brother, and, well, we ain't seen any money from it. Just the new rifles. We been thinkin' there should be something more for us."

"What about the bank robbery?" Carr barked. "You got two hunnerd apiece after that, didn't you?"

"We did," Jamison conceded, "but that was a while back. We all know there was a box of cash on that train, and you been holdin' that real tight. We ain't seen none of that money, and it don't seem right."

Jamison held Carr's stare, and the others stepped in beside him. Carr stared back at them, his brain racing. He couldn't take out all three, not at once. Not that he didn't believe in himself with his Colt. He had downed that gunfighter at the ranch in Fredericksburg, hadn't he? Still, three at once...

Carr fought down his rising anger and decided he had to make the peace. "Okay, two hunnerd apiece more, from the cash on the train." He stared at the hardened faces in front of him. He could see that two hundred wasn't enough. "Three hunnerd, and that's it. That's half of what we took," he finished, lying smoothly.

Jamison and the others exchanged looks. They knew there was more money in that box on the train, but they weren't sure how much. Three hundred, in addition to the bank robbery loot, was more money than they had seen. Harris and Blondie gave Jamison a slight nod.

"Okay, three hunnerd," Jamison agreed.

"Okay," Carr growled, turning back to stare at the fire. The other three didn't move.

"What?" Carr barked. "What now?"

"We need the money now," Jamison said.

Carr lifted his eyes and stared at Jamison. His hand moved just slightly toward his Colt, then relaxed. He was sitting, and they were standing. There were three of them. He would find a way to get that money back later.

"Fine," Carr snarled. He rose and turned to his saddlebag, resting close behind him on the ground. When he opened the bag, he used his body to shield their view. He reached in, counted out nine hundred, and gave it to Jamison.

Carr watched them out of the corner of his eye as they retreated and split up the money. He would push them as hard and far as the men and horses could go tomorrow. He really needed to reach the Roost in two more days.

———

I said my goodbyes to Julia and Pete at the doc's office, where Pete was getting checked out one last time. I went to get their horses and mine at the livery stable, then came back to the doc's office to see them off. McNelly had already told me he didn't intend to arrest Pete for his part in the robbery and train wreck, so I told him his only job was to go home, get well, and stay away from Elmer in the future.

Julia whispered a thank you and gave me a kiss. When they had given me a last wave and headed south to Fredericksburg, I went to the train station.

McNelly had good news for everybody. The Rangers were paying for the train tickets, and McNelly gave us fifteen dollars apiece for the trip, also courtesy of the Rangers. McNelly took me aside and gave me a telegram he said came in answer to one he had sent yesterday.

I sat down on a bench at the station and read the telegram:

> Leander McNelly,
> I am Lieut. Pike Hardy. I will meet you
> in Becknell, NM, in six days. Stop.
> I will bring six troopers with me. Also a
> Surprise to help with the rock fortress. Stop.

I folded up the telegram and gave it back to McNelly. "I wonder what the surprise is," I mused.

McNelly pocketed the message and took a seat on the bench. "Me, I've always been kinda partial to artillery," he chuckled.

The train rolled in with cinders flying and brakes squealing. Boone seemed to have his doubts once it came down to boarding, and he was mistrustful of giving his horse over to a handler to load on a car. I pointed out that the horse couldn't get on and ride with us in the passenger car. Eventually he quit grousing and got on the train with me.

I figured we had several days in front of us, just riding on the train. I hoped it would be worth it.

CHAPTER 19

PIKE AND NAPOLEON

To say that Becknell, New Mexico, was any more than a speck in the trail would be giving it too much credit. Boone and I stood in the middle of town, trying to shake off the dust of the trail. I imagined once in a while I could still feel the train bouncing and swaying down the tracks.

Still, we had made it here in six days, arriving about midday on the sixth day. I saw a saloon that had three horses out front, making it the busiest place in town. There was a general store, which had everything you could need, according to the sign above the door. Boone and I stopped in there for a minute and decided that was true, if you just needed beans, bacon, or maybe a little ammo.

There was a place called Ma's café, but I didn't feel hungry enough to give it a try. I was wondering what we were going to do around here for the next day or two until Lieutenant Hardy showed up. McNelly lifted his hand and pointed down the trail. There was a small cloud of dust out there, getting a little bigger as I watched.

Another fifteen minutes and we could see the dust was coming from a column of troops. Ten minutes later, they rode into town. Most of the dust was caused by a cannon being towed behind the soldiers. A rangy, dark-haired soldier swung down and walked up to me. "Captain McNelly?" he asked.

"Sheriff Jake McCabe," I answered. "You're Pike Hardy, right?" I returned his handshake and pointed over to McNelly. "That's McNelly over there."

McNelly talked with Hardy for a minute, then motioned to me, and I came over with the map we had found in Wagon's saddlebag. Hardy leaned over the map, his face eager. He scanned it from all angles, his finger tracing a line along the middle of the map.

"What's that you're tracing?" I asked.

Hardy straightened and held out the map so we all three could see it. "I'm just tracing with my finger where the Santa Fe Trail dips into No Man's Land," he said, repeating the motion with his finger while we watched.

"I've chased some outlaws south from the trail right about here," he said, pointing to a spot just north of the Roost on the map. "They always lose me after a few miles. I'm bettin' this is where they went," he said, tapping the spot where Carr had marked the Roost.

Hardy took off his hat and ran his hand through his hair. "This map shows how to get to the Roost from the north," he observed. "From here, the most direct way is to come in from the west." He replaced his hat and looked from McNelly to me and back. "Knowin' how hard it is to find from the north, and what with hauling ol' Napoleon over there..." He grinned and pointed at the cannon. "Maybe the best thing would be to come in on a direct line from the west, seeing how we've got this map to help us along. I could guide us in on a route just south of the Santa Fe Trail."

That made sense to me. I nodded at McNelly, who agreed. "Let's do it," he said.

Hardy looked overhead at the sun, then back at the map. "I'd guess if we leave right now," he said, "we'll pull in there around sundown, which would probly be the best. Otherwise, they could see us from that shelf where the fortress is. For sure, we want to get Napoleon set up after sundown. That needs to be a surprise in the morning."

"Okay," McNelly agreed, "how long will you need to set up Napoleon?"

Hardy beckoned to one of his men. "Hostler!" he barked.

A young man looked up and walked over to us. He looked about fifteen, but I'm sure he was older. He was skinny, and I couldn't help but stare at his Adam's apple, jumping up and down every time he swallered, which was a lot of swallers.

"Hostler," Hardy said, "how long will it take to set up Napoleon and get a good idea about the range?"

"One hour, sir," said Hostler, gulping twice more. He saluted and walked away.

"Don't worry," Hardy said, watching McNelly and I stare as Hostler left. "Hostler, there, can destroy that rock fortress in no time once I turn him loose with Napoleon."

McNelly and I pulled ourselves together and decided to take Hardy's word for it. "Okay," I said, "that gives us not much time before we pull out. There's water your men could pump for themselves over there by the water trough. Food over there, I guess," I said, my voice trailing off as I looked at Ma's café.

Hardy laughed. "I'm from the backwoods of Arkansas, and I've et most things you can imagine," he said, "but the boys and I vowed never to eat at Ma's café again. We been here before, we have, and my stomach ain't forgiven me yet. I'll stick with the biscuits and jerky in my pack."

Thirty minutes later, we moved out, Hardy and the troops leading the way because they were most familiar with this area. McNelly, Waters, Boone, and I brought up the rear. If Carr was out there, I promised myself he'd be answering to me soon.

———

Johnny Carr brought his men into the Roost as promised, and only a day later than he'd expected. This latest batch of horses they'd stolen had been ridden so hard he wondered if they would ever recover. Never having ridden in from Texas before, he promised himself he'd be taking the train route from now on.

Tempers were boiling to the point of mutiny, so even Carr had the sense to lay off for the next day. Looking around at some items in the Roost and checking the animals grazing in the canyon down the trail told him that Dennison had pulled a robbery on the Santa Fe Trail against orders, but he would let that pass, too.

The morning after arriving, he sat down at the table with them after some coffee and breakfast. Dennison, he had to admit, was a pretty decent cook.

"Boys," Carr said, "you've all got a little money from our Texas trip, except for Dennison, but it looks like he made himself a little money while we were gone, too.

That's all good. We need to rest up for a little while here."
He shot a glance at Dennison, who avoided his eyes.

"Maybe," he continued, "while you're resting, I'll go
over to Santa Fe and buy some things to stock up a
private saloon here." He glanced around the table—that
had gone over every bit as well as he'd hoped.

"After we're all feelin' good, we can work some of the
ranches and settlements over in New Mexico. We ain't
been over there yet. And after that, when things have
settled down in Texas, maybe we'll see what we can do
down in Dallas and Ft. Worth. We'll ride the train both
ways, I promise. No more humpin' it up that trail for a
week and more."

Hearing a little buzz around the table and sensing a
better mood than before, Carr got up and left them. He
didn't want to keep all of them around here, but there
were ways of putting one man in more danger than
others during a robbery. He could get rid of one or two
that way. He could pick up a few others when he needed
them.

Carr went down the hall to the room he kept for
himself in the Roost. He worked the lock he'd put on the
door and looked in his bag. Between the bank robbery
and the train robbery, he had about $2,500 left for
himself. He would spend a few hundred on stocking a
saloon, like he'd promised. He pulled out about four
hundred for booze for the saloon and some spending
money for himself. He grinned and stuffed that money in
his pocket. The rest he put back into the bag. He would
not spend all his time in Santa Fe stocking a saloon.

Carr felt the rock wall of his room for the loose
rocks he knew were there. He pulled them out and
stuffed the bag with the remaining money from the

robberies into a little nest behind the wall. He would come back later and see how much he had in his secret spot after putting in the latest money he'd just added to his stash.

———

We pulled to a stop at dusk. I had been looking through my field glasses at a long bench of rocky land in front of us. I stopped and focused in on a large rock structure halfway along on the bench. Surprised at the size of it, I blurted out the first thing on my mind.

"We found it," I said, more excited than I thought I'd be. "That's got to be what Carr is calling the Roost."

I passed the glasses around, and one by one, the others agreed with me. I looked over at Hardy with even more respect than I had started with. He had kept the Santa Fe Trail on the left as we came in, then veered south when he thought we were getting close. And there it was, right in front of us, right when he'd said we would be here.

"Nice job," I said. The others all mumbled agreement.

Hardy nodded and looked off to his left. "I think, since we've agreed to split up and cover this place from north and south, that I should take the troops and old Napoleon up there to the north side. I think we can get in closer from there."

Nobody felt like questioning his judgment at this point. "Do it," McNelly said, speaking for all of us. "We'll set up to the south. I expect they'll come piling outta that house to the south side once a cannonball or two hits 'em from the north."

"We'll attack at dawn, starting with the cannon,

right?" I said, just reminding everybody what we had already agreed on.

Hardy tipped his hat and started to move his men away. "Oh, Lieutenant," I said. Hardy stopped and looked back. "That first shot," I said, "when Hostler's trying to get the range. He'll send that one in short on purpose, right?"

Hardy grinned and nodded. "That's right," he agreed. "I know you boys don't want no cannonballs bein' served up for breakfast."

We moved around to the south of the ledge, finding a small ridge about one hundred yards to the south of it. I could see a trail or two worn into the side of the ledge, where men and horses had climbed up to the house.

I studied the rock house through my field glasses in the fading light, looking for the doors. There was only one main door in the middle. I swung the glasses left and right. My gut told me that Carr wouldn't come out of that house with the others once old Napoleon made things too hot to stay in there. My gut told me he had a hidey-hole, someplace to make a secret escape.

The shelf sloped more gently off to my right. There were more trees and vegetation off on that side. When McNelly, Waters, and Boone began spreading out and finding a spot to bed down for the night, I told them I wanted the right flank. I didn't tell them why, and nobody seemed to have a problem with it.

I nibbled on a little food, but I wasn't that hungry. We all bedded down early for the night. I took one last look at the Roost before I rolled up in the blankets. Carr was going to answer to me tomorrow morning.

I was awake before dawn, but I could sense that gray early morning light not far away. I lay on the blanket until a few fingers of light began creeping up on me from the east, filtering through the trees. I stood, rolled up my blankets, and slung my gun belt around my hips.

I couldn't see the others off to my left. If they weren't up yet, I knew they would be soon. Hardy had proved himself to be a man of his word. The hostilities were just about to get started. Just a few minutes later and I could see Boone, he was sprawled out in front of a log, sighting down the barrel of his new Winchester. I grinned for just a second—he was like a kid with a new toy.

I heard a little whistling noise in front of me. It grew louder with each passing second. I hunched down in the little hole I'd carved out for myself last night and pulled a log in front of me. A few seconds later, there was a tremendous crash out on the other side of the rock house, maybe a hundred yards down the far side of it. In my mind, I took off my hat to Hostler. He didn't look like much, but the boy could shoot a cannon.

Carr was feeling pretty good about things as he left his room. He grabbed a burlap sack and headed for the pantry. He was looking forward to his trip to Santa Fe. He just needed a few vittles to get him there. Carr opened the pantry door, frowning when he saw his choices. Maybe, he thought, he would take a packhorse with him and bring back a little food for the pantry.

Stepping out of the pantry, Carr froze when he heard a sound he hadn't heard since the war. Unfortunately, he'd heard way too much of that noise back then, and he knew exactly what it was.

"Cannon!" he shouted. "Cannonball coming in!"

The others were standing next door in the kitchen and they froze, mouths open, not believing what they were hearing. There was a gigantic explosion and crash. The ground under them shook. Pots rattled and fell off their hooks on the wall.

"Cannon!" Carr shouted again. "Coming from that way!" He pointed to the north, then shouted again, pointing south this time. "Get out of here! Front door! That way!"

They sprung into action now, running into each other, clawing and fighting to get out.

"Rifles!" Carr shouted. "Grab those Winchesters!"

Carr didn't stop to see what they did. He couldn't see where Dennison was, but he didn't have time to worry about that. He ran toward the east side of the house, stopping to pull aside a large baggage trunk resting against the wall at the back of the hallway. With the trunk out of the way, he could see the passageway leading out of the house and toward the canyon where the stolen livestock grazed.

Carr dashed back to his room, yanked the rocks from the wall, and pulled his money from its hiding spot. Running back to the hallway, he heard the whistle of another cannonball. He ducked into the secret tunnel, hunched over, and ran as fast as he could.

————

Dennison chose not to go out the front door with the others. He had a few reasons for not doing that. One, he didn't trust Carr. The man lied to his face more than anybody Dennison had ever met. Two, he considered it highly likely that there were guns along that ridge to the south. Their attackers didn't have to be a bunch of geniuses to figure out that men would run out on that side, trying to get away from that cannon. And three, he'd been in the war, too. He'd seen what an exploding cannonball could do to a man in an open field.

No, thought Dennison, he would take his chances inside these rock walls. He caught sight of Carr running toward the south side of the house. Dennison's lips curled in disgust, and he moved the other way. He stopped in front of the stone fireplace. This, he thought, was as much protection as he would find around here. Little did he know that Hostler had sighted in on the chimney.

There was that whistling noise again. It was louder this time. Dennison dropped to his knees in front of the fireplace and covered his head with his hands. At the last minute, he knew how close this one would be. Dennison sprawled flat on the floor, his hands still over his head. There was a crash so loud he looked up just in time to see the entire chimney blown apart. Huge stones were headed right at him. Then the world faded away.

———

The second shot crashed into the house. I ducked down behind the log on pure instinct, but it turned out I didn't need to. The rocks flying off from that house were landing a good fifty yards short of us. I raised up to look at the destruction. It looked like Hostler had scored a direct hit on the chimney. The house caved in, starting in the middle, followed by both sides collapsing inward.

Three men made it out of the house just in time. The first two collided in the doorway, fought each other off, and plunged out, followed by the third man. The first two were carrying rifles. All of 'em were headed directly toward us, trying to get away from that cannon.

McNelly let them get within rifle range. When they were less than a hundred yards away and climbing the slope toward our ridge, McNelly half-rose and shouted through cupped hands:

"You men! It's the law! Stop where you are and throw down your weapons!" The two in the front raised their rifles and got off one shot apiece. There were four answering shots from the ridge and they dropped to the ground, dead as soon as they landed.

The third man stopped where he was, hands above his head. "I got no gun!" he shouted. "I surrender." He dropped to his knees, his hands still raised in the air.

There were three men below me, two dead and one alive. I didn't know how many had been in the house. One look at the house convinced me there was nobody alive in there. Hostler and old Napoleon had knocked it flat. I grabbed my field glasses and looked at the three men who had come out of the house. Carr wasn't down there.

CHAPTER 20

ME OR HIM

I stared at the foot of the ridge, using my field glasses to focus in tight on the three men down there. McNelly, Boone, and Waters had reached the base of the ridge now. Waters used his boot to turn the two dead men on their backs. Boone and McNelly stood the prisoner up on his feet. I could see them all clearly. Carr wasn't there.

Putting down the field glasses, I looked across at the collapsed rock house. Nothing was going to come out of there alive. If Carr was trapped in there, I could figure he was dead. Unless he got out somehow before it had come down. Feeling panicked, I remembered the sloping ridge on the right side of the fortress. I picked up the field glasses and peered over to the right of the rock house. Nothing. Unless...I swung the field glasses back and forth. There were branches moving over there.

I grabbed my Winchester and hit the slope in front of me, half-running and half-slipping to the bottom, where I got my footing again. I followed the ravine, running toward the collapsed right side of the rock house. I heard a shout from Boone behind me, but I couldn't spare a second of time. I waved my right hand over my head, still running down the ravine.

I reached a spot just about even with the edge of the rock house. The ravine curved in a little closer there, and I lost a lot of time scrambling over the rocks that had landed after Hostler and old Napoleon did their work.

I jumped out of the far side of the ravine, scrambled over some logs, and trotted around what had been the east-facing wall of the house. I dropped down onto a faint trail leading away from the pile of rock, then stopped and stared behind me.

There was a tunnel coming out of the shelf, just below what had been the wall of the house. I stooped down and gawked into the tunnel. The wall of the house may have concealed it before, but the wall of the house had caved in. The tunnel collapsed, maybe halfway along from where it had started, assuming it had started under the edge of the house. I turned and looked down the trail, sloping down and curving away from the house. I saw tracks there. Fresh tracks.

I started running down the trail, but after I rounded the first curve, I realized that Carr or anybody else could be out there, perched behind a tree and waiting to dry-gulch me the minute I came around the bend and gave them a first-class target. I dropped to a crouch and moved to the side of the trail, following the tracks and looking for any movement I could see out in front of me.

————

Carr ran to the end of the tunnel, lunging the last few feet. The crash behind him was deafening, and the ground shook beneath him. He could hear the tunnel collapsing, the sound was building as it roared in his direction. Carr dove and hit the ground just outside the tunnel, rolling to get farther away. Dust billowed out of the tunnel in a cloud, covering his clothes and his face. He coughed and sputtered, getting to his knees and stumbling away from the wreckage behind him.

Looking into the tunnel, or what was left of it, he figgered he had made it with maybe thirty seconds to spare. The tunnel was halfway collapsed. Coming to his senses, he realized he could be found and shot out here at any minute. He broke into a shambling run, shoving aside the tree branches that overhung the narrow trail.

Rounding the first bend and pulling up in his tracks, he looked down and realized he had left his Winchester rifle in the house. He had hung on to the money bag, but he'd left his rifle after telling the others to take theirs. He cursed himself loudly, then stopped abruptly, looking around wildly in all directions.

Forcing himself to calm down, he looked down and saw, with relief, that his pistols were intact. Both of the double-tied-down Colts were there—he hadn't lost them diving and rolling out of the tunnel. He checked, both were loaded, and he had more ammunition in his belt. He turned and trotted down the center of the trail, dodging the overhanging branches this time and pacing himself.

It was a mile down to the canyon. If he trotted all the way, he could make it without stopping. He had a head start—no reason to think anybody would catch him from behind. Nobody would be fool enough to run down the center of the trail where he could pick them off. He reached the canyon pasture about ten minutes later, shooing the five cows and three horses to the back of the canyon, up against the rock face.

Carr circled the pasture, deciding where to hole up. There was a boulder about halfway between the rock face at the back of the canyon and the mouth of the trail leading out. He would like to have the rock face right behind him, but he was too open if he just stood in front of the wall. Anybody could bring him down with a rifle shot.

To his left, there were elm trees guarding the entrance to the pasture for about one hundred yards on that side. Carr considered burrowing down in those trees. The problem was, he wouldn't have a clear view of the mouth of the trail. He decided to shelter himself behind the boulder, out in the middle of the pasture, for the first two hours. If nobody came during that time, he would curl up for a rest in the elm trees, then take one of the horses and make his way out of here under the cover of darkness.

Carr moved behind the boulder. It offered ideal protection, shielding him in front about halfway up his chest. He pulled the Colt from the right-hand holster and laid it on top of the boulder. He kept his hand next to it, watching the trail like his life depended on it. It actually did depend on it, he knew that.

———

I stayed in a crouched position, trotting in the places where the trail went on a straight path. When I approached a bend in the trail, I took to the trees at the side, cat-footing it up to the bend and checking the trees in front for any sign of a dry-gulcher. I was mindful at all times of the tracks—they were still there, leading right down the center of the trail. The distance between tracks told me he was keeping to a pretty steady pace. This was a man with a destination in mind.

I kept it up for about a mile, I figured, until I slipped through some elm trees at the edge of another bend in the trail. Looking through the trees, I could see that the trail was opening up into a pasture, probably a small one, but there was some grass out there.

I stayed in the trees, crouching low and easing forward. When I could see the pasture directly in front of me, I dropped to my knees, crawling on from tree to tree until I could see the whole pasture. It was a small one, probably couldn't keep more than a dozen cows fed at a time, but what got my attention was a boulder in the center of the pasture, just a little to the left of the center.

Carr was behind that boulder, there was no doubt about that. I could see his face clearly. I watched for a while longer until I could see the pistol he had resting on top of the rock. He was expecting company, and he didn't plan to be a good host, I could see that.

Right then, I was thankful for all the time I had spent as a kid in Kentucky, crawling through the trees, trying to sneak up on a deer for a good shot. I was a little bigger now than I was in those days, but my woodsman skills hadn't left me. I took off my boots so I could feel the ground under me, wishin' I had my moccasins. No matter, I moved back about five yards to keep the trees between me and him. Me and him, I thought, this is how it's gonna wind up.

I spend about fifteen minutes working through those trees, first drawing even with him, then slipping behind him. As I got behind him, I was aware of the horses. I didn't need a snort from one of them alarming him. I crawled over to the edge of the pasture and I stepped out behind him.

There was a twig in front of me. I pulled my Colt from the holster, trained it on Carr's back, and stepped on the twig on purpose. He froze where he was for just a second, then turned his head ever so slightly. His right hand edged toward the pistol.

"Uh-uh," I said. "You don't wanna do that. I've got a gun on your back right now. If you reach for that pistol any more'n you have already and try to spin around, the last thing you're gonna see is my face while you slide down to the bottom of that boulder."

"Jake McCabe," he said softly. His head turned a little farther, but that hand stayed still. He had a left-hand gun too, but he held his left hand well away from the gun. He laughed softly, but it was one of those laughs where you know there was nuthin' funny going on.

"I guess I knew this might come down to me and you," he said, just loud enough for me to hear. "I hear you're pretty slick with that Colt, that's what I hear anyway. I'm not so bad, myself. Jake, I can't believe you'd shoot me in the back. How about you give me a fair chance, just for old time's sake?"

I watched him suspiciously. "What have you got in mind, Carr?" The words came out of me in a low hiss.

"You let me holster my gun," he said. "I'll lift it high and slow, where you can see it. Then I'll drop it in my holster and turn around real slow with my hands in the air. After I do that, you holster your gun and we'll have us a fair fight. Just you and me."

I took my time thinking about it. This, I decided, was something Julia would never know about. "Okay," I said, still suspicious. "You do it just like you said, and you'll get that fair fight you're wanting."

He did it just like he said he would. The left hand stayed well away from the gun in his holster, and he moved ever so slowly with the gun from the top of the boulder. He lifted it high, raised his left hand in the air, and turned around as slow as can be. He dropped the gun into the right-hand holster and stared back at me.

I dropped my gun into the holster and watched him like a hawk. I'd been in one man-to-man gunfight before in my life, and it was the eyes that gave him away. I didn't so much as blink, just watching those eyes.

Carr focused on a spot just to my left and behind me. A puzzled expression came across his face. "Wagon?" he asked. "What're you doing here?"

It was the oldest trick in the book, and I fell for it. Well, mostly I fell for it. I knew Wagon was dead, but Carr didn't know that. By the time I had it sorted out in my head, he had moved. His hand had flashed down to his holster, and the gun was coming up.

My hand dropped down to my Colt and I cleared leather faster than I ever had in my life. His gun boomed, and I felt a burning slice of pain across my left side. I leveled my gun and fired the first time, aiming for the center of him. He gasped as the bullet caught him in the belly and slammed him back against the boulder. He dropped his gun, then clawed at the left-hand gun, trying to bring it up. I fired again, and his left front shirt pocket disappeared, driven right back into his chest. His lips moved, but he didn't say anything, just stared at me as he fell to the ground.

My words turned out to be true. The last thing he saw was me as he slid down to the bottom of the boulder. I held my gun for a long time, just staring at him, trying to convince my brain that this was over. Finally, I put the Colt back in the holster.

"I guess you got what you wanted," I murmured. "Just me and you."

I was feeling weak, and I dropped onto the grass. I checked my side. The bullet left a trail across it, but it didn't look serious. He had just creased me, but it hurt, and I knew it would hurt for a while. Then I heard a familiar voice.

"Jake? You in there?"

It was Boone. I waved my hand in the air.

"Jake? You in there? I got a scattergun over here," the voice continued, "and if it ain't Jake McCabe in there, I'm gonna use it on you. And there's two more boys behind me, just to clean up any mess I leave behind. Speak up!!"

I realized I was behind the boulder. Boone hadn't seen me wave.

"Boone," I shouted as loud as I could manage. "It's Jake. All good. I'm behind the boulder. Carr's dead."

Boone trotted out of the woods at the side of the trail. He kneeled down beside me and inspected the wound. "You'll do," he observed. "You got somethin' for Julia to fuss over, while you play the hero an' all."

He rose and went over to take a look at Carr. "He's got some big leaks, he does," Boone observed. He stood and shook his head. "I reckon you're gonna tell me I gotta bury this coyote," he said. He sighed and went looking for something that could serve as a shovel.

McNelly and Waters came a few minutes later. I trailed behind while they dragged the body out. Hardy had a detail at work, digging a grave for the other two we had shot earlier. They rolled the three bodies into a shallow grave and walked away. They trussed up the one called Harris like a turkey and marched him over to a horse.

I walked over to Hardy and shook his hand with a nod at Hostler. "You ever get over to Texas, down near Fredericksburg, I hope you come and say hello," I said.

Hardy grinned, saluted, and waved as the soldiers left, taking Harris with them.

I was feeling a little weak, but I worked my way to my feet and walked over to mount up on Sherman. I took one look back at the rock house as we rode out. It was nothing but a pile of rubble now.

CHAPTER 21

BOONE'S SURPRISE

I opened my eyes and looked around. I knew where I was. The big ranch house had a guest bedroom, and I was in it. At Julia's house. Well, Ike and Jeanne's house, along with Julia, Pete, and Isaac. The door opened and Julia peeked around the corner.

"Ah, you're awake," she said, coming in to straighten the sheets. She sat down on the edge of the bed and leaned in to give me a kiss. "You must have lost a lot of blood," she said. "You were pretty wobbly when you got here, and talking kind of funny. Funnier than usual," she said.

I chuckled, and she smiled that beautiful smile. "You still have your sense of humor," she observed. "I think you're going to be fine."

The door swung open a little farther, and Boone came in, holding hands with Alice Brenham. "I knowed it," Boone announced. "You're gonna milk that little scratch for all it's worth." He stopped and drew himself up to his full height. "I got some news," he boomed.

I just lay there and waited. I had a feeling I knew

what was coming, but I couldn't quite believe it. "Me and Alice are gettin' hitched," he thundered. "She done said Yes. Can you believe it?"

"Uhh..." I mumbled. I started to ask Miss Alice if Boone had held a gun to her head, but Julia was giving me a warning look. "I, uh, well, that is a surprise," I said, still mumbling. I looked over at Julia and remembered my manners. "Congratulations to the both of you," I said, coming out of my shock just a little.

"I think it's great," I said, knowing that I was rambling. "It's great that you'll have each other while you're still, uh, young, and have good health." I glanced over at Alice Brenham. "And you've both still got good eyesight and all, I guess."

Julia made a show of straightening up one of the pillows, leaning over me. "You be nice, Jake McCabe," she whispered, giving me a tiny little pinch on the cheek for good measure.

"I wish you the best," I said, recovering my manners just in time. "When is the big day going to be?"

"Haven't decided yet," Boone hollered. "I guess we gotta talk about that next." He was on such a cloud he hadn't even noticed my crack about Alice's eyesight. They sailed out of the room. I waved goodbye and slumped back down on my pillows.

Julia settled back down on the side of the bed. "There's something I want to talk about," she said, taking my hand.

"Okay," I told her. I had a feeling I knew where this was going, and I didn't mind. We probably needed to have had this talk back when I left for No Man's Land, but there just hadn't been any time.

Just then, Julia's father Ike came and sat down on the

side of the bed. "Got a minute?" he asked, looking at me first, then Julia.

"Sure," Julia answered. She looked at me. "Can I get you anything?" she asked.

"I've been hankering for some coffee," I said. "Do you have any?"

"I'll make some," she answered, pulling the door closed as she left.

"You doin' okay?" Ike asked. "McNelly said it was just a crease but kinda deep."

"Fine," I assured him. "I'll be up and bothering you in no time."

Ike laughed and laid a hand on my arm. "Do you remember," he asked, "the first time I asked you to come to dinner at our house, back there in Kentucky?"

I thought back and smiled. "Sure, I remember," I said, thinking back. Mostly, I remembered how it felt like family there, just after the war. And, I remember Julia, no more than seventeen, but I thought she was just about the prettiest, sweetest girl I had ever met.

I look back at Ike. "It scared me to come, on account I knew my table manners were terrible. Most times back at home, I didn't bother with a fork or spoon."

Ike had another good laugh, then turned serious. "This guy Carr, he's gone, right?" Ike said. "He won't never be back to bother my family?"

"I shot him back there," I said. "Twice. We buried him in No Man's Land. I didn't say any words over him, on account of I had nothing good to say, but we sure enough buried him."

"You gave him all he deserved and more," Ike said fiercely. Then his voice softened, and he gave my arm a pat. "What I come to tell you," he said, "is that night when I invited you to have dinner with my family, back there in Kentucky? That's one of the smartest things I ever done in my whole life."

Julia came back in as Ike left, giving me the coffee and looking back at Ike as he left. "Everything okay?" she asked.

"Good," I assured her. "Everything is great."

She brightened up and snuggled up to my good side. "What I wanted to talk about," she said, "is well, Boone and Alice are getting married, and we've agreed for a while we're going to get married, and I wondered..." Her voice trailed off.

"You're wondering when we're going to get married," I finished, reaching out to take her hand.

"Yes!" Her face blossomed into that beautiful smile again.

"When were you thinking about doing that?" I asked. "When do you want to get married?"

The door came open suddenly and Doc Reagan came in. I glanced over at Julia, thinking she must have asked him to check on me. I braced myself. Doc was nicer to me than he was to Boone, but he didn't like patching folks up after they got themselves shot up, as he liked to tell me.

"Got yourself shot up again, did ya?" Doc said as he advanced on me, putting some kind of device on his head.

"Well, not on purpose or anything," I said defensively. "I mean, he was shooting at me and everything."

"Hmmmph," he said, leaning over me to haul up my shirt and have a look at the wound. He inspected it for a while, poked and prodded me a couple times, listened to my heart, and put his hand on my head. Finally, he lifted my coffee cup, sniffed it, and again said, "Hmmmph."

"I reckon he'll be fine," he announced to Julia. "Assuming he don't go and get hisself shot up again." He moved toward the door.

"Dr. Reagan?" Julia said, stopping him at the door. "How long do you think it will be before Jake is back to being himself again, up and around and all?"

"About two weeks, and he'll be back to normal," Doc Reagan said. "As normal as Jake gets, I mean," he said over his shoulder. Then the back door slammed, and he was gone.

Julia came back to sit down on the bed. She took my hand. "In answer to your question," she said, "I was thinking about getting married in two weeks."

"Two weeks," I repeated. A small smile popped up on my face, then it spread into an ear-to-ear grin. "Two weeks it is."

A Look At Book Three
McCabe's Land

Some men fight for justice—Jake McCabe fights for everything he has.

As sheriff of Fredericksburg, Texas, Jake McCabe has faced his share of trouble. But nothing prepares him for what rides out of the hills next. When a Comanche uprising threatens to ignite the frontier, the Texas Rangers come calling—and McCabe answers.

But danger doesn't just come from the wild. An old enemy, long thought buried in McCabe's past, returns with a vengeance, setting his sights on Jake's land, his family, and everything he's built.

Outnumbered and outgunned, McCabe must rally a few loyal friends and draw a hard line in the dust. Because in Texas, land is more than property—it's legacy. And some things are worth dying for.

AVAILABLE AUGUST 2025

ABOUT THE AUTHOR

Patrick Lindsay came to Texas by way of Missouri, Canada, and California and has been proud to call the Lone Star State his home for more than forty years now. He retired in 2017 from "another life" as a CPA, whereafter he turned his hand to writing.

He has read just about everything by Louis L'Amour and first decided to give Western writing a try on his initial day of retirement. He has been writing ever since and loves the idea that so many people get enjoyment from his work.

Patrick and his wife Michelle live on a cattle ranch near Fort Worth along with cows, horses, chickens, and a very spoiled Great Pyrenees dog. He is an avid fan of the St. Louis Cardinals in baseball and the Kansas City Chiefs in football.